OVERW

S0-AVF-546

DEADLOCK
REBELS

OVERWATCH®

DEADLOCK REBELS

BY LYNDSAY ELY

Scholastic Inc.

© 2021 Blizzard Entertainment, Inc. All rights reserved. Overwatch and Blizzard Entertainment are trademarks or registered trademarks of Blizzard Entertainment, Inc., in the U.S. and/or other countries.

All rights reserved. Published by Scholastic Inc., *Publishers since 1920.* SCHOLASTIC and associated logos are trademarks and/or registered trademarks of Scholastic Inc.

ISBN 978-1-338-74036-3

1 2021

Printed in the U.S.A.   23

First printing 2021

Book design by Jeff Shake

Cover illustration by Xiao Tong Kong

CHAPTER 1

The thing about trouble was, once you got into its company, it was tricky getting out. You could try to avoid it, you could run from it, you could even fight it—which was, in the case of the Bonney brothers, exactly what Ashe had done—but it still had a way of finding you.

"I don't even know what to say, Elizabeth." There were crumbs in Sheriff Carson's mustache. Only a few, but enough to draw her eye, distracting remnants of the man's breakfast. "Am I ever gonna see the last of you?"

"I told you..." Ashe clenched her teeth, fingers worrying at her silk skirt. A few hours ago, it had been immaculate. Now it was wrinkled and stained with spots of blood. Not hers, of course. "It was self-defense. *They* attacked *me*."

The sheriff sighed, loosening a few of the crumbs and sending them plunging to the screen displaying Ashe's record. "That's not what those boys say."

"Well," she locked eyes with him, "then they're liars as well as bullies."

But the sheriff didn't believe her. She could see it on his face, plain as the crumbs. Not that his skepticism about her innocence was unexpected.

The only surprise was how fast this day had managed to go from bad to worse.

It had started so good, too.

For once, Ashe woke with the sunrise, raring to go. Most days began with B.O.B., her family's robot butler, yanking the blankets off her five minutes before she needed to be out the door. An advanced, sentient omnic, B.O.B. had been by Ashe's side for as long as she could remember, acting as both a companion and a bodyguard. And, of course, making sure she got up for school in the morning. But she didn't need B.O.B.'s help today.

Because today was special. Today was graduation day. Not only did that mean she'd never have to set foot in the suffocating halls of that tedious, soul-sucking academy again, it meant she'd get to see the look on Headmaster Wallach's weaselly face as he handed over the diploma he never thought she'd get.

The same looks she hoped to see on her parents' faces as she walked across the stage.

Ashe washed, dressed, and brushed her snowy hair until it shined. Then she took the steps of Lead Rose Manor, her family's ancestral home, two at a time as she went downstairs to the formal dining room, where her parents always ate breakfast.

But when she reached it, the room was empty. No steaming cups of coffee, no holovids projecting endless financial reports and sales figures, no parents.

Only a vase of stark white roses on the mahogany table, and a card leaned up against it.

Congratulations, Elizabeth! We're so proud of you!

Despite the warm words, Ashe turned cold as she read, the color leeching out of the room until it was as hueless as the roses.

We know we'd promised to be there today; however, an exciting business merger called us away at the last minute. But we're very proud of you, and hope you'll see this as a fresh start, a moment in which to leave behind the missteps and troubles of the past and finally embrace our family legacy.

They hadn't even taken time to sign the card.

Ashe frowned. *"We're very proud of you . . ."*

It read like a joke. A bad one. If they were so proud, why weren't they here? Why had they left her alone, *again*?

Family legacy. What a joke. Across the room, the portrait of her great-great-and-more-greats-grandmother Caledonia stared blankly down at her. It was Caledonia who'd created the Arbalest Arms Company, who'd built the foundation for the premier, high-tech arms dealer it was today. Not Ashe's parents, who preferred to rub elbows and chase deals with the executives of more powerful corporations—Helix, Vishkar, Hyde Global, and the rest—trading on a reputation whose success they had little to do with.

If anything, they'd gotten lucky. Arbalest had done good business for years as the makers of expensive, highly customized luxury rifles. But then the Omnic Crisis happened, and the military turned their attention to them. Arbalest's AA92 rifle became standard-issue for the army due to its higher capacity and higher muzzle velocity. With that contract, demand for their unique brand of rifles exploded. War was good for business.

Especially if it was far away.

Larger cities had been hit by the war, sure, but Bellerae, the community where they lived and where Arbalest was based, was secluded. Before the crisis, they'd never had more than a dozen omnics to speak of. It had remained mostly untouched throughout the war, during which the company's factories kept up brisk production.

But now the crisis was over, thanks to Overwatch. Demand for weapons was down; already one Arbalest factory in Bellerae had closed. Ashe's parents were more interested in business deals made and executed thousands of miles away than in the community their company had kept thriving for generations. What kind of legacy was that?

Mounted below the painting was an heirloom Viper rifle, one of Arbalest's early creations, and the gun that had carved the company's place in the weapons market. Over a century old, the gun still looked new and shot straight. Innovation. Quality. That was the legacy Caledonia had strived for, never letting Arbalest lag behind, hiring the best and brightest minds she could find, and always making her workers feel valued—more like family than employees. Not that she was a pushover; it was said she made her employees call her Ms. Ashe, no matter how long they'd known her. Maybe it was meant to show respect. Or maybe she'd simply disliked Caledonia as much as Ashe disliked Elizabeth, also preferring to be called by her surname.

Ashe turned as a clunking tread approached. In the doorway of the dining room stood B.O.B., a tray balanced delicately between his massive metal hands. On it was her favorite breakfast—waffles dripping with syrup and a big side of bacon, extra, *extra* crispy.

A sour taste rose in her throat. "Do I look hungry right now?" she snapped.

The omnic simply blinked at her and placed the tray on the table. Immediately, Ashe felt a pang of guilt. B.O.B. hadn't done anything wrong. In fact, he'd been the only dependable part of her life. Except, of course, during the war, when he'd disappeared. Like all omnics, he disappeared during the Omnic Crisis. Years passed, during which Ashe thought she'd never see the butler again. It had surprised her how much she missed the omnic when he was gone. Then, after the war had ended, he returned to Lead Rose, newly sentient and . . . different in ways Ashe never entirely understood. But he was still the companion she remembered. And he'd stuck by her side ever since.

Unlike her parents.

"They could've at least said good-bye." Her voice caught on the last word, and she tensed, as irritated with herself as she was with them. This wasn't the first time her parents had left her alone with hardly a word, and it probably wouldn't be the last. As far back as she could remember, there was only the sprawling, echoing solitude of the estate—especially during the years of B.O.B.'s absence—or else the tense veil of her parents' disapproval for whatever mess she'd gotten into lately.

She twisted the card in her hands. So why was she so steamed?

Because today was supposed to be different. Her graduation had actually seemed to mean something to them. Maybe they'd only wanted to show, in public, that their daughter was more than a troublemaker. More than the girl who'd gotten caught trying to convince the academy's resident hacker to change all her grades to As, or caused the school to close for decontamination after showing off with her slingshot in the science lab. Or maybe, as Ashe had hoped, it was a reason for them to finally believe she was capable of doing something right. She'd sworn to graduate. And they'd promised to be there.

Fool that she was, Ashe had believed them.

On the table, the roses caught a ray of morning sun, lighting them up like a bead drawn on a target. That's what she wanted to make of their peace gesture right now—to set it in her sights and watch the gift explode in a spray of petals and crystal. If the Viper had been loaded, she might have.

Instead, Ashe dropped the card on the mantel and stomped toward the hall. As she brushed by B.O.B., he reached an arm out, stopping her.

Ashe sighed. "Don't worry, I'm still going to the stupid ceremony!"

B.O.B. cocked his head.

"No, don't get the car. I'd rather walk . . . alone."

The omnic held up a hand in warning.

"I know, I know. That's not allowed." But Ashe didn't feel inclined to follow any rules right now. "But before we leave, can you go find my gold bracelet? You know, the one my parents sent for my birthday last year? I forgot to put it on."

B.O.B. turned obediently, heading upstairs. Normally, the butler would escort her to the school. But right now, Ashe wasn't in the mood for company. Which meant distracting B.O.B. with a little white lie. By the time he realized the bracelet was nowhere to be found in her room (Ashe's mother had borrowed it months ago and never given it back), she'd be long gone.

Ashe took the path to town that followed along the river. As hoped, it was deserted, save for some ducks and the occasional police surveillance drone. But despite the quiet solitude, her mood remained sour. And it wasn't as if she could call up a friend to commiserate with. Her status as the daughter of the powerful Ashe family had kept her peers at a distance for most of her life. More recently, the closing of an

Arbalest factory had resulted in a number of her classmates' families losing jobs. For a few of them, casual avoidance had given way to active dislike, leading to more schoolyard scraps than she could remember. The graduation ceremony, and her escape from the academy, couldn't come fast enough.

Still, beneath the ornamental stands of terraformed trees running along the water's edge she could breathe a little easier. Forget, for a moment, the stifling loneliness of the estate and pretend that she was somewhere—and someone—else entirely.

"Well, well, what kind of early bird do we have here?"

Ashe stopped, her calm immediately gone. She turned, already knowing who she'd find trailing her: Jodie and Jimmy Bonney. A year behind her in the academy, there was no one in Bellerae who hated Ashe and her family more than these two. Both their parents had worked at Arbalest for decades, only to be unceremoniously dismissed when the factory shut down.

"Why, Jodie." Jimmy chuckled. "I do believe that's the rare scarlet-eyed peacock. Strange; usually this bird is accompanied by a big, clunky butler-bot."

Great. These two goons were the last thing she needed. "Run along, boys. I'm *not* in the mood."

"No need to be tart," said Jodie, trading a mischievous grin with his brother that Ashe didn't like. They might be younger than her, but they were a lot bigger. "After all, you're graduating today, aren't you? Congratulations! But tell us the truth: How much did your parents *donate* to make that happen?"

Ashe bristled, but kept her stare cool. "Don't know. Probably a heck of a lot less than it would take to get Headmaster Wallach to pass the head-scratching, paste-eating pair of you."

The Bonneys' faces darkened in unison.

"You think you're so clever," Jimmy sneered. "Having a fortune doesn't mean you get to talk down to us."

Ashe's blood warmed, flush with rising adrenaline. "Oh, boys"—she gave them a mockingly patient smile—"I could be poor as dirt and still talk circles 'round *you*."

It was the wrong thing to say, and yet, she couldn't stop herself. She was brimming with frustration, and if the Bonneys were foolish enough to set themselves in her path, so be it.

Jodie's voice took on a sharp edge. "Poor as dirt, huh?" He reached down and pulled up a clump of soil. "We could give you a taste of that, couldn't we, Jimmy? Let's make this peacock a little less pretty for her party."

Ashe straightened, still smiling. Two against one? Not the worst odds she'd had.

Jimmy charged forward, attempting to grab her, but he was slow in more ways than one. Ashe danced out of reach, kicking him as she did. Jimmy yelped as her foot connected with his shin, sending him sprawling in the grass.

A hand clamped onto her forearm. Jodie—quicker than his brother—yanked her toward him, trying to subdue her with a bear hug. But she dropped at the last moment, driving a shoulder into his gut. He gasped and lurched back, the wind knocked out of him. Nearby, Jimmy scrambled to his feet, face red with humiliation.

"You done?" Ashe spat. "I ain't got all day, y'know."

With a roar, Jimmy advanced again, fists flying. She ducked one punch, then another—wild haymaker swings that would have rattled her gears if they'd landed. But Ashe knew how to dodge a punch.

And how to throw one. She waited for an opening, then—

Her fist jabbed out, catching him in the mouth. Jimmy went to his knees, blood pouring over his lips.

"You—" It was Jodie who spoke, the words low and icy. "Now we're gonna make you *a lot* less pretty." Suddenly, silver flashed in his hand.

A knife.

Ashe took a nervous step back. Maybe it had been a mistake to bait the boys like she had. There was brawling, and then there was this.

But Jodie left no time for de-escalation, or reason. Eyes glossy with anger, he lunged. She sidestepped, grabbing at the wrist holding the weapon while simultaneously throwing an elbow up. It found his nose with a satisfying *crunch*. As Jodie joined his brother on the ground, the knife slipped from his fingers. Ashe snatched it up, brandishing it as she backed away from the pair.

That's when the sirens started. A pair of Bellerae police hoverbikes appeared, lights flashing. Realizing one of the passing police drones must have caught sight of the scuffle, Ashe turned, but a third police officer was already behind her.

"Don't move!" The deputy dismounted, rifle trained on her.

Ashe swore, and dropped the knife.

So much for getting to graduation.

"My deputies found you holding a weapon," continued Sheriff Carson, scowling, "and both those boys bleeding, swearing you attacked them."

"I know how it looks." Ashe practically sugarcoated the words, smiling as innocently as she could manage. It wasn't easy, not while thinking about strangling the Bonneys for their lies. "If you would let me—"

"Enough!" The sheriff slammed his fist on the desk. "It's always some excuse with you, Elizabeth. You think you can do what you please, and then use your last name like a shield."

Ashe scoffed. "That isn't tr—"

"Well, not this time," he spat. "Get up!"

"What?"

He grabbed her arm and hauled her to her feet.

"Hey!"

"Maybe if you have some time to reflect, you'll learn a little humility." The sheriff dragged her out of the office and down the hall to a musty, dimly lit part of the station she'd never seen before.

The jail cells.

"Oh, come on, Sheriff," pleaded Ashe. "This is completely unnecessary. Call B.O.B. He'll be here in a jiffy—"

"Oh, I know." Sheriff Carson unlocked one of the cells and shoved her in, a satisfied little smirk tugging up one side of his mouth. "Your parents' money to the rescue *again*, and no one to say 'boo' about it because they own half the town. Well, this time I'm in no rush. And you're underage, which means you can't post bail on your own. So, I'll get to that call . . . eventually. But not until you finally get a look at the inside of a cell."

The door slammed shut.

"Wait, please—" Ashe tried, and failed, to stay calm as he strode away. "Dammit, Sheriff, you get back here!"

But he ignored her. Ashe wilted as he disappeared,

hanging on to the bars of the cell. The sheriff wasn't going to listen. He *never* listened. Like everyone else in this godforsaken town—her parents included—he'd already decided who Ashe was . . . who she was always going to be. A spoiled heiress. A troublemaker. A threat to their pride.

And it didn't matter if she thought different.

"Huh . . ." A voice came from behind her. "You've got an awful lot of grit for a rich girl."

She twisted toward the sound. "*Excuse* me?"

One cell over, a lanky form reclined, feet up on the bench set into the wall, a hat pulled low over his face. "A *rich girl.* Gotta be, with that swanky outfit." His voice was deep, smooth.

"Mind your own business."

He snickered. "What made you fancy a look inside a jail cell?"

Ashe narrowed her eyes. "I didn't *fancy* a damn thing. I don't belong here."

The hat pushed up, revealing a young man with a ready smirk and piercing brown eyes, one of which was bruised and swollen. "Funny. Me neither."

"Oh, really?" Ashe scoffed. "That shiner indicates otherwise."

"This?" The young man sat up, fingers raised to the bruise. "Friend of mine had a little . . . misunderstanding with another farmhand. I stepped in to settle it."

"Can't help but notice you're alone in there."

A shrug. "He's had a few too many run-ins with the law already."

Her annoyance turned to surprise. "You—you took a beating *and* an arrest for him? That sounds awful generous. And more than a little stupid."

"Like I said, Julian's a friend. Don't have a lot of those to spare." The young man stood with a slow, sinewy stretch. "What about you? How'd you get thrown in here?"

"Same story," Ashe replied carefully, reconsidering him. He couldn't have been older than she was—maybe younger, even, though there was an air about him that told her he'd seen more than his share of the world already. "A misunderstanding."

"Then I guess we've got something in common"—he approached the wall of bars that separated their cells and stuck a hand through—"Miss . . . ?"

She hesitated, but only for a moment. The thing about trouble was, once you were familiar with it, it was easy to spot. And next to the Bonney brothers, this boy looked like a friendly puppy.

She took his hand and shook. "Call me Ashe. And you are?"

"Name's Jesse." His grin widened further. "Jesse McCree."

CHAPTER 2

"**S**o," said Jesse, hanging on to the bars between their cells. "Sounds like the sheriff really has it out for you."

Ashe rolled her eyes. "Let's just say we've crossed paths before."

"Well, I've only recently become acquainted with him."

Ashe went over and sat on the narrow, suspiciously stained bench in her cell, her only option besides the floor. "I take it you're not from around here?"

Jesse shook his head. "Got to town about a couple months ago. Been working over at the Ace Valentine megafarm. Not exactly glamorous, but it's better than an empty stomach."

Ashe knew the farm, though she'd never been there. The

chaos of the Omnic Crisis had displaced millions of people, and many of them were looking for a new place to settle, or at least steady work. Bellerae, surrounded by a number of sprawling corporate farms terraformed into the desert landscape, had drawn its share. "Where were you before?"

"Oh, here and there. You know how it is."

She didn't. "You don't look much like a farmer to me."

That seemed to amuse him. "I do what I have to." He paused. "Could be worse, and it has been. Working the railway would be better, but Ace Valentine isn't so bad."

"Except when you're getting into fights?"

He chuckled. "Like I said, a misunderstanding."

"Mhmm," Ashe said, nearly rolling her eyes.

"Julian bet the other farmhands I could shoot a playing card from fifty yards." He tilted his head back with a grin. "They didn't much care for losing that wager."

Ashe sat up a little straighter. "You shoot?"

"Since I was a pup." Jesse's eyes narrowed, as if he saw the meaning beneath her question. "You?"

She shrugged noncommittedly. "I've been known to dabble."

Jesse's mouth tugged up on one side. "You any good?"

"I wouldn't want to ring my own bell"–she felt a smile forming on her lips, too–"but *only* fifty yards? Wouldn't even be a challenge until at least a hundred."

"Sure, but the folks Julian made the bet with didn't know that," he said. "Revolver or rifle?"

"Rifle," said Ashe. "Accuracy is key. One shot should be all it takes."

"Maybe if you're shooting clay pigeons at a lawn party," Jesse teased. "Prefer a revolver myself. Faster, and you can shoot from the hip if you need to." He sighed. "But the sheriff took my revolver. It wasn't much—a cheap piece of iron—but it shot straight. Won't be moving on until I can get ahold of a new one. It's dangerous out there, on your own."

"I wouldn't know. I've been stuck here most of my life." Her parents had access to both a private jet and their own personal car on the transcontinental railway. Not that they'd ever taken her anywhere with them. "You headed somewhere in particular?"

"Nope." Jesse straightened. "Maybe the coast, eventually, get some work in security. I might be able to shoot the moon down now, but nowhere will have me on for another few years."

"I know the feeling—being overlooked for no good reason, that is. But if you shoot like you say you do, it's their loss." Ashe felt a tug of something in her gut, caustic, like . . . jealousy? True, Jesse might be a drifter without a penny to his name, but he had a certain kind of unencumbered freedom, the ability to make his own decisions about what he did, where he went. Dangerous or not, it held an allure. "So, Jesse McCree, it looks like we're going to be stuck here for a while. And I've never been anywhere but here. So tell me what it's like, what it's *really* like, out there beyond Bellerae."

". . . and that's why I don't eat pork anymore."

Ashe barely heard the end of the story over her own laughter. She leaned forward, sides aching from it, and wiped a tear away. "And did he ever find his boot?"

Jesse, reclining on the bench once more, shook his head. "I wasn't sticking around to find out!"

"Can't blame you." Another peal of laughter escaped. "If I'd gotten my hands on you, I would have—"

A metallic *clunk* cut her off. Ashe looked up to find the sheriff in the door of her now open cell, looking as stone-faced and unamused as ever. She hadn't even heard him approach.

"That's it, Elizabeth," he said, with a faint hint of annoyance. "You're out."

"What?" she said.

"'Elizabeth'?" said Jesse.

"You heard me. Surprise, surprise, the charges have been dropped *again*. C'mon." The sheriff stepped to one side, clearing the way for her.

Automatically, Ashe stood, exiting the cell. Jesse stood as well, making his way over to the bars, looking a little disappointed. Or maybe that was her imagination.

He tipped his hat. "Nice meeting you, Ashe."

"You too, Jesse." It was all she had time to say as the sheriff hustled her to the entrance of the police station, and then out into the street.

At the bottom of the building's steps, B.O.B. stood beside one of the family's sleek black town cars, holding open the door. It wasn't an unfamiliar sight. And yet, something about it made her itch with apprehension.

"Bailed out again," spat the sheriff. "The Ashe family special."

She ignored him, wordlessly descending the steps and sliding into the car's back seat. She felt the vehicle dip and rise again as B.O.B. took his specially modified seat in the front, and then they were moving, leaving the police station behind.

Ashe leaned her head back and let herself melt into the soft leather seat. She wanted a bath. And those waffles she'd left behind earlier. And maybe an hour or two to shake the strange feeling meeting Jesse McCree had left her with, one that she'd never experienced—

"*ELIZABETH CALEDONIA ASHE!*"

Her mother's voice screamed through the vehicle as the holoscreen burst to life in front of her. Suddenly, both her parents were glaring at her, from the balcony of whatever ridiculously posh apartment or hotel they'd set themselves up in this time.

"I didn't have the knife," Ashe snapped, automatically. "Those idiots pulled it on *me*, I was only defending—"

"Whatever excuse you have," her mother interjected, "I don't want to hear it." Her eyes were aflame in a way Ashe had never seen before.

Even her father, who excelled at consistent indifference, had red blooms of anger coloring his cheeks. "Honestly, Elizabeth, haven't we put up with enough? We've given you every advantage—yet you still find trouble every chance you get."

Ashe crossed her arms and looked away. Sure, they'd done all that. Usually from halfway across the continent. Still, she felt a twinge of guilt at the disappointment in her father's voice. Today was supposed to have been a day for them to be proud of her.

"And after all that," her mother continued, "after everything we've given you, you go ahead and allow something like *this* to happen."

The screen changed, and suddenly Ashe was staring at herself on the front page of the local newspaper, the *Bellerae Daily Pioneer*.

"Arbalest Heiress Arrested for Armed Assault," the headline above her picture read. And below: "A history of violent outbursts and unhinged behavior!"

Ashe groaned. What newspaper didn't love a good scandal? It wasn't even a good picture. Blurry and tilted, it showed her grimacing, with a line of blood running from her nose. Definitely from the academy, probably snapped by one of her classmates during a scrap. It was effective, though. She looked like a mad dog.

"How could you?" her mother hissed, white teeth showing behind too-red lipstick. "Do you know what people will say if this gets beyond Bellerae?"

The guilt disappeared. So that's what this was about. Not what had happened to her, but rather how it might make her parents look to all their stuffy friends. "That I shouldn't be messed with?"

"It's not funny!" Both her parents were red in the face now. Her father shook his head with frustration and disappeared from the frame, but her mother remained. She closed her eyes, taking a deep breath before speaking again. "This is the last straw, Elizabeth. Nothing we've done so far has been getting through, so it's time for drastic measures. You're turning eighteen in three months. When that happens, you're cut off."

Ashe turned cold.

"Do you hear me?" her mother continued. "You will be disowned. No credit lines, no nice home, no butler to cater to your every need. Nothing. You want a life of privilege again, you're going to have to get it on your own."

The cold turned to sick numbness as the blood drained from her cheeks. "Mother, I–"

"I told you, I don't want to hear it! You've had every chance in the world, and you've squandered them all. Well, not anymore." Ice frosted her mother's words. "Three months, Elizabeth. That's about how long our business will take here. When we return, your days of having it easy are over. Do you understand?"

No! she wanted to scream, at the top of her lungs. She was their daughter, and they were going to disown her because . . . because they were *embarrassed*? "None of this would have happened if you'd kept your promise to come to my–"

"Do you understand?" Her mother was gone and in her place was the businesswoman who negotiated with some of the most powerful people on the planet. A woman who knew when to give ground, and when to hold it.

And Ashe knew she wasn't budging. "I . . . understand."

"Good. Then I suggest you spend the last few months of your time at home thinking about how you've gotten yourself to where you are, and try to come up with a plan for something better."

The holoscreen disappeared.

No good-bye. No hint of remorse or affection. It was as if Ashe had become a bothersome product to be scrapped, an undesirable deal to be dissolved.

For the rest of the ride home, she felt completely, utterly, empty.

CHAPTER 3

*B*ANG!

The vase burst into a multicolored cloud of porcelain and enamel. Ashe moved her sights to the next target, a crystal decanter from her parents' personal study, balanced on a wooden fence post.

BANG!

Shards of crystal glittered in the air as whatever priceless vintage that had filled the decanter seeped into the estate's lush green grass. How much destruction had she tallied up by now? A hundred thousand dollars? Two hundred thousand? Antique china, marble sculptures, dusty wine bottles—older than her parents, even—one by one they met their fate at the business end of her rifle.

Disowned.

BANG!

DISOWNED.

The word ricocheted through Ashe's thoughts, hitting every raw part of her until her mind felt sore all over. How could they do this, toss her away like she was nothing? Like she was disposable? It's not like they had any other children they'd spent years ignoring. Who was going to carry on the family legacy now?

Ashe scoffed at the thought. It had never been about anything as sacred as a legacy. All her parents cared about was their precious image, and how it could help them rise in favor among the world's elite. That was the most important thing to them, more than their legacy, or Arbalest.

Or her.

BANG! BANG! BANG!

They did care, however, about the various collections of art and wine they had amassed. How else would they advertise how much money and taste they had, those times when they were actually home long enough to throw parties at Lead Rose? Those trinkets had been the only outlet for her anger that Ashe could think of after she'd gotten home from jail. All night, she stewed over what her mother had said to her, what her father hadn't, and what was going to happen to her after she turned eighteen in a few months.

Where would she go? How would she get by?

Bellerae certainly didn't want her around, that much was clear. And she didn't have any money, not really; only a few limited lines of credit that B.O.B. had access to, just enough to cover her basic needs.

At least her parents remembered that she needed to eat.

Ashe raised the rifle again, but this time when she pulled the trigger, nothing happened.

Empty.

B.O.B. reached out, handing her more rounds.

Ashe waved him away. This wasn't nearly as satisfying as she'd hoped. "That's enough of that." She blinked at the sudden, frustrated burning in her eyes. No. She wouldn't cry, not for them. Sure, she'd gotten into trouble here and there. But she was also smart, and she was ambitious. They'd just never been around long enough to see it. "Not like it means a damn thing anyway. They'll only buy more."

Because vases and wine were replaceable. So was art and fancy china and antique rugs and everything else that filled the halls of Lead Rose. Her parents had so much, they probably wouldn't even notice if half of it disappeared one day. The one thing that couldn't be replaced—her—was the only thing they didn't care about.

Ashe stared at the shattered remains of the decanter, mesmerized by the *drip, drip, drip* of its contents. She could shoot up every nice thing on the estate, and it wouldn't matter in the end. There was no real revenge in rampant destruction, even if it—briefly—made her feel better.

But maybe there was somewhere else.

An idea began to form. Her parents might be willing to kick her out, but that didn't mean Ashe had to go empty-handed. At first, she considered selling Lead Rose's various fancy whatnots and pocketing the profits, but the market for those items were limited and would require very specific buyers. She'd never have enough time to arrange the sales. But there were *other* markets, and *other* goods she had access to. Arbalest made all sorts of things that the black market would kill—literally—to get their hands on.

Ashe smiled. In the privacy of their own home, her parents were never as careful with their passwords and systems as they should have been, and more than once Ashe had "borrowed" them for her own use. Like when motorcycles with lev rims first came out, and Ashe just had to have one. Her parents had been baffled when they'd returned from a trip to find her buzzing around the grounds with it, but she'd managed to convince them it had been a gift sent by some business associate or another, and she'd lost the card.

These days, Ashe had access to just about everything her parents did: Arbalest company's systems, inventories, and shipping schedules . . .

What had Jesse McCree said about how dangerous it was to travel outside the bounds of Bellerae? The Crisis may have been over, but all sorts of gangs roamed the countryside these days, and robberies were common. A few more wouldn't be anything of note, even if they happened to be unusually focused on Arbalest shipments.

Ashe smiled for the first time since she'd spoken to her parents. They thought she was nothing but trouble. So, she'd be trouble . . . for them. She'd take what she wanted from Arbalest, sell it on the black market, and start her new life using the profit. She was heir to the Arbalest fortune, after all. She had a right to her inheritance.

But she couldn't do it alone. Even with her parents' credentials to get her started, hijacking Arbalest shipments wouldn't be as easy as ordering a hovercycle off the internet. And as intimidating as B.O.B. could be, he wasn't exactly the ideal partner in crime. No, she'd need someone clever, reliable, and looking to fill their pockets.

Luckily, she knew someone who fit that bill perfectly.

"B.O.B., get the car," said Ashe. "We're going for a ride."

Ace Valentine. That's the farm where Jesse had said he was working. Ashe knew it, though not well. It was owned by one of the farm corporations who'd made their way into the area after the Omnic Crisis, using terraforming technology to change the land and scale production to fulfill the demands of the ravaged country. Her parents had consulted for a few of the corporations, even invested in them. Farms weren't as profitable as the weapons business, but if there was one thing folks always needed, it was food.

Squared-off fields flew by the car window—corn, wheat, orchards with their neat rows of fruit trees. All surrounded by three-story-high electric fences that sent a very clear message to any drifters or displaced persons who might pass by: There were no free meals at the Ace Valentine industrial megafarm.

The car turned in at the farm's entrance, following a road that led to a cluster of stark, utilitarian administration offices. Beyond it were warehouses and other industrial buildings—produce could go from the field to the processing equipment to packaging in a matter of hours, ready to be shipped out by the fleet of trucks Ashe spotted off to one side.

Ashe had B.O.B. stop a little way from one of the buildings, a rather dour square of painted concrete with a sign that read HUMAN/OMNIC RESOURCES over the front door. Off to one side of it, a small crowd of people were gathered. It took only a glance to figure out who they were—folks looking for whatever kind of work might be available today: equipment maintenance, putting in irrigation lines, even picking the more delicate crops the automated systems had trouble with. Half were barely Ashe's age; all looked like they could use a few more meals than they were getting. A cloud of fatigue hung over them, along with a sad sort of hopefulness, especially in the gazes locked on the front door of the building. Had Jesse looked like that, when he first arrived?

"Wait here, B.O.B.," said Ashe.

Her plan was a simple one. After all, who was going to question why the daughter of the two most powerful people in Bellerae was asking for some random farmhand? No one knew how far she'd fallen in her parents' favor. Not yet. For now, if she asked for a two-headed neon green rattlesnake, they'd jump to try and find one for her.

But as it turned out, Ashe didn't need to ask anything of anyone. The moment B.O.B. opened the car door for her, the door of the human/omnic resources building flung open as well, and out stumbled Jesse McCree.

A large, red-faced man followed on his heels. "I don't care what you *think* you did, kid, you're done here!"

Too caught up to notice Ashe, Jesse turned back to face

the man, a deferential set to his stance. "Look, Mr. Doherty, this was all a misunderstanding that went a little too far."

"Too far?" cried Mr. Doherty. "You put *three* of my workers in the med clinic."

Jesse stood a little taller. "They would have done the same to Julian if I hadn't—"

"Oh, your little friend? He's gone, too. I'm surprised you had the guts to even come back here after that mess." Mr. Doherty's frown deepened. "You think I need this? Need workers like you?" He jabbed a finger at the gathered crowd. "No, I do not. Because there's always someone waiting to take an open place. Someone who won't cause trouble. Now get out of here before I set the security drones on you!"

Jesse's shoulders slumped as Mr. Doherty stalked away toward the hopeful workers, all of whom were now trying to get his attention.

It was a sorry sight, but one that suited Ashe's intentions just fine. "Hey! McCree!"

He turned, disappointment melting away as he spotted her, revealing the self-assured young man she recalled from the jail cell.

Ashe smirked at him. "Need a ride?"

Jesse tried to play it cool in the car, especially after seeing B.O.B., but even he couldn't keep the astonishment out of his face when they pulled up to Lead Rose Manor.

"You gotta be fooling me." His mouth hung open like a fish's. "I figured you for a rich girl, but you live *here*?"

Exist might have been a better word than *live*, but Ashe nodded. "Home sweet home."

"So . . ." Jesse's gaze moved to her. "What exactly does your family do, Ashe? Or is it Elizabeth, like the sheriff—"

"You call me Elizabeth, and I'll give you another black eye to match the one you already have. And my family owns a little weapons business. That's all."

She hadn't told him much during the ride, instead focusing on the rest of his story. The sheriff had finally released Jesse after a long night sleeping on a bench in the cell, sending him on his way with a stiff back and no revolver. And though Jesse had headed immediately back to the farm, Ashe had seen the result of that.

"Didn't even get my last week's wages," Jesse had said bitterly. "After all, who was I gonna complain to? The law?"

Jesse followed Ashe out of the car when B.O.B. opened the door for them, but paused when she headed away from the manor and onto the grounds. "Not going to show me around?"

"Not yet, farm boy." She curled a finger at him, indicating he should follow. "I wanna see something first."

Ashe led him to the crest of a hill that overlooked the estate, where the remains of her earlier "target practice" were still scattered across the grass. She'd had B.O.B. set up two new sets of targets along a fence about a hundred yards away—two sets of six wine bottles each.

Jesse took in the scene and then cocked an eyebrow at her. "We having a party?"

"Of a sort. B.O.B.?"

The omnic stomped up the hill behind them, a revolver in one hand and a rifle in the other. He presented Jesse with a revolver. It was an older Arbalest model, nothing fancy, just something Ashe had dug out of one of the manor's storerooms.

But his eyes went wide. "This is a really nice—" Jesse stopped. Looked from the revolver to the rifle, and then down at the mansion again. "Hold on. When you said 'little' weapons company. . . did you mean *Arbalest*?"

"Compared to the corporations, it's small."

"Uh-huh," said Jesse. "What exactly are we doing, Ashe?"

She smiled. "Performing a test." Ashe pointed to the right-hand set of bottles. "You say you're a good shot, McCree. Prove it."

At first, she didn't think he was going to bite, but Jesse

McCree didn't strike her as someone who backed down from a challenge.

And she was right. He took the gun from B.O.B., looking from it to her and back. Then, quick as lightning, he spun and fired.

On the fence, the first bottle in the line exploded.

"Not bad." Ashe held out a hand to her butler, who filled it with the rifle, another one of her storeroom finds. She raised it, taking a split second to line up the sight, and then pulled the trigger.

A moment later, her set of bottles matched Jesse's.

"Not bad, yourself," he said. "'Course, it would be way more impressive to see how fast you could take the rest of those down."

Ashe knew a dare when she heard one. She moved as quick as he did, each of them squeezing off five more shots. Within moments, not a single wine bottle remained standing.

"Hah! Beat you by a hair," Ashe crowed.

"I don't know about that," said Jesse, looking smug. "Pretty sure I got my last target first."

"Why don't we ask B.O.B.? He'll know for sure."

"Or we can call it a draw"—Jesse turned a sharp eye on her—"and you can tell me what's going on here. I'm starting to worry you plan to hunt me for sport or something."

He said it with humor, but Ashe rolled her eyes. "I have . . . a proposition for you."

"A proposition?"

"Yes," said Ashe. "But first, that tour you wanted." She started down the hill, pausing when he didn't move. "I'm not gonna hunt you for sport, I promise."

Jesse still looked skeptical, but he shrugged. "You'd never catch me, anyway."

Ashe led him back to the mansion, making sure they entered through the spectacular main hall, with its soaring rotunda and crystal chandeliers. This was followed by ornate parlors, a tearoom filled with masterful stained glass, the stunningly stocked library, and, finally, the dining room. Jesse's head moved like he didn't know where to look next, eyes wide at the glut of paintings, antiquities, and fine furniture.

"Everything you see here was paid for by the profits from Arbalest." Ashe gestured at Caledonia's portrait. "The company built by my ancestor Caledonia. My parents run it these days and, until yesterday, I was their only heir."

That pulled Jesse's attention back to her. "Until yesterday?"

She nodded. "In three months, I turn eighteen. When that happens—thanks to my recent troubles with the law—my parents are going to cut me off, completely and forever. All this . . . gone."

Confusion filled Jesse's face. "So, what does that have to do with me?"

Ashe crossed her arms. "I'm not giving up my inheritance without a fight. Before then, I plan on fleecing Arbalest for all I can, stealing its goods and selling them, and leaving here with enough money to go wherever I want and do whatever I feel like. And I want you to help me."

"Me? Why?"

"Because you're a good shot," she replied. "You need money, too, and it sounds like you have at least some loyalty to your friends."

"Sure," Jesse said carefully. "To my friends."

Ashe smirked. "Would ten percent of the take be enough to make us friends for the next few months?"

For a moment, he simply stared at her, expression unreadable. Then he looked around at the surrounding luxury again, no doubt trying to calculate how much ten percent might be. "I don't know," he said finally. "Sounds like this could be dangerous."

"You afraid of danger?"

"Didn't say that. Just want to know why you think you can pull this off."

Ashe gave him a patient smile and began to unload her rifle. "I've got Arbalest inventories, shipment manifests, and the administrative access to schedule my own, if I want," she said as she worked. When the magazine was empty, she handed the rifle back to B.O.B. "Everything I need to know to pull off a string of profitable heists. All I need is some help. And when it's all said and done, we can go our separate ways, with enough funds to start lives anywhere we want to go."

Jesse's gaze landed on the portrait once more, and then the Viper below it, lingering there. He took a long breath and let it out before turning back to her. "I want twenty percent."

She would have gone to thirty. "Okay, but I have one more condition. Whatever we do, we do it my way. Understand?"

His eyes narrowed a little as he considered her. Then he nodded. "You're in charge."

"Then we have a deal." Ashe held out her hand.

Jesse took it, and they shook.

CHAPTER 4

"So, just curious," Jesse said, keeping his voice low, "what would you say if I were having second thoughts about this?"

They crouched on a ridge ten miles from Bellerae, hidden in a rocky outcropping. Below sat the Arbalest Fulfillment Center Beta-3, its windowless black warehouses arranged in a neat grid. The last time Ashe had seen this place, it was through a car window and during the day. Now it lay in shadows, light from the thick slice of moon in the night sky glinting off the security drones patrolling the electrified perimeter fence. She didn't know what McCree was worried about; from what she saw, this was going to be a cakewalk.

"I'd say you better find your backbone quick." Ashe adjusted her Panoptica field glasses—an Arbalest elite accessory in limited edition onyx black—to get a closer look. A data overlay updated in real time over the current night vision view, funneling her measurements of distance, topography, wind speed, and more. "And get ready, because if we're going to pull off any heists, we need better equipment than I can scrounge up at home. We need what's in *there*."

"You said you could get us inside, no problem." Jesse took the field glasses from her and peered through them. "That fence looks like a problem. How are we supposed to get over it?"

"Don't need to." Ashe grabbed his arm, pulling him closer and pointing. "Look." A small, overgrown structure sat five hundred meters from the complex, concealed by a swell of hill. "That's our way in."

Jesse cocked his head. "A shed?"

"That's what it looks like, huh? B.O.B., send that schematic over." Behind them, the omnic tapped Ashe's tablet, and a moment later Jesse gave a low, impressed whistle. She knew what he was seeing—the same overlay she saw, of the tunnel below the shed, leading all the way to the warehouses. Arbalest might be a legitimate business, but that didn't mean they didn't need to do some discrete moving of goods now and then.

"Under instead of over, huh? I suppose that could work."

Jesse's gaze dropped. "You planning on leaving that there?"

Ashe looked down. Her hand was still on his arm. She drew back, scowling, as he gave her a cheeky grin. "You planning on coming, or not?"

She started down the ridge, not waiting for a reply. A moment later, she heard him follow. As if he'd seriously miss out on this. She'd seen the spark of greed in his eyes as she described the heists she had planned for them. That is, if they could pull off tonight. He wanted this as much as she did. More, maybe. They both had a chance here—her to use the Arbalest tech that should have been hers to set the stage for a new future, him to escape the go-nowhere life of a farmhand.

They moved briskly, near invisible in dark gray dusters and hats, Ashe's hair tucked carefully into hers. They'd left the old utility truck they'd "borrowed" from the estate back in the brush, stripped of all registration markers, physical or digital. B.O.B. was a little more difficult to conceal, but he could move surprisingly lightly for two tons of metal, and there was no surveillance in this area to worry about. That tidbit of information was courtesy of the same security schematics that had informed her about the existence of the tunnel.

Up close, the concrete shed was perfectly deceptive, its metal roof rusted and weather-stained, the weeds waging a winning battle up its walls. If Ashe hadn't known the exact spot beside the gray metal door to press, she might have thought they were in the wrong place. But she did, and a panel slid open, revealing a hidden digital keypad. All she needed to do was enter the access code plucked from her parents' files, and they were in.

"Wait." Jesse grabbed her wrist as she reached for the numbers.

"What? Now's not the time for cold feet, McCree!"

"It's not that." Jesse let go, his face serious. "It's only . . . Once we do this, it can't be undone. You've barely given your parents a chance to cool off. What if they change their minds, huh?"

Ashe tensed. She'd expected more of his unwarranted hesitation. Not this.

"You've got a lot to lose, Ashe. More than I've got to gain. You sure you're ready to throw that away?"

If this went right—and it would—they'd be set up to make more money than he'd ever known. And he was worried about *her*? Indecision bubbled. Maybe he was right. Maybe in a week, or a month, her parents would reconsider, forgive her, and bring her back into the fold. She was, after all, their only child. At some point they might remember that.

And then what? Ashe's resolve rose like a tide, washing away the doubt. As long as she was part of the family she'd been born into, she'd be at its mercy, under its yoke. A piece in whatever games her parents would want her to play, ones that she had no control over. She'd been to enough of their soulless parties and tedious dinners filled with sycophants or whoever else they thought could get them another rung up on the social ladder. No more.

"Jesse McCree, I may not be able to see the future," Ashe said quietly, "but I know one thing: Whether I'm headed for heaven or for hell, I want it to be on the route that I choose. Not one chosen for me. So, are you with me or not?"

For a moment, there was nothing but the buzz of night insects.

Then Jesse grinned. "Like I said, You've got an awful lot of grit for a rich girl. Let's get a move on."

Ashe returned the smile and tapped in the passcode. With a hiss of hydraulics, the door popped open.

"B.O.B., you stay here," Ashe ordered. The omnic wasn't going to fit through the entry, anyway. "Stay out of sight, and shoot me a heads-up if you see anything awry."

The butler moved to the shadowed side of the building, his optics fading to a low glow.

Inside, the shed was nothing like the outside. Automatic lights came alive as they entered, revealing metal walls and a grated floor. The egress point for the subterranean cargo platform was set in the center, but Ashe passed it by and went to a hatch set in the floor. Another code opened that with ease, revealing a long vertical shaft with ladder rungs set into the wall.

Jesse leaned over it, peering down. Even with the goggles, the bottom was out of sight. He swallowed hard. "Ladies first."

"Ain't you the gentleman?"

Ashe began the descent. The air was cool but musty, as if no one had opened the hatch in a while. After a few yards, the shaft opened up, joining up with the space that would be occupied by the cargo platform, still currently below. They'd need it on the way back, but for now this seemed safer.

About fifty meters down, they reached the bottom of the shaft. The cargo platform was to one side of them; on the other, a corridor that led in the direction of the warehouses.

"See?" Ashe cocked her head at Jesse. "So far, so good."

"Sure," said Jesse. "But let's not jinx it."

"Anyone with a good enough plan doesn't need to worry about jinxes. C'mon."

They traveled along the corridor in silence, though its discrete purpose meant there were no sound or movement sensors down there. She could have screamed her lungs out without worry. Which wasn't as comforting a thought as it could have been.

"Peaceful down here," Jesse whispered.

"Sure, just like a tomb." Ashe checked the schematic again. "A little farther, then we take a left."

Sure enough, they reached a split. Not far beyond that was a faint glow of light: the end of the tunnel. And then . . .

The warehouses were as deceptive on the outside as the shed had been. Jesse gave a low whistle as their eyes adjusted to the wan light, and a massive chamber opened up before them. Towering shelves full of black cargo cases soared stories above, interconnected by a spiderweb of metal walkways.

"So, all this would've belonged to you?" Jesse turned in a slow circle as he took in the room. "How are we going to find anything in this horde? Should I, uh, start opening crates or something?"

"Watch and learn, farm boy." Ashe pulled out a tablet she'd brought from home, loaded with her parents' restricted files. Moments later, a warehouse drone whirred its way toward them, stopping to hover a few feet away. "Our little friend here will fetch what we need. Just give it a shopping list, and an admin code—which I have, of course."

She queued up her father's personal code in the tablet and hit SEND.

"Incorrect authorization." A single red light lit up on the drone like the angry eye of a cyclops. *"Please try again. Mandatory alert triggered in ten . . . nine . . ."*

Ashe frowned. It should have worked; her parents' access was absolute. She sent the code again.

"Incorrect authorization." The drone moved away a few feet, as if readying to go for reinforcements. *"Eight . . . seven . . ."*

"Uh, Ashe . . ." Jesse took a step back. "Everything okay?"

"Yes!" No. She chewed at her bottom lip. Everything was definitely not okay.

"Five . . . four . . ." The red light began to pulse menacingly.

Jesse drew his revolver. "I was kidding about the jinx, y'know."

"Put that away and stop distracting me!" Ashe's fingers hovered above the tablet, trembling.

"Two . . ."

She entered a different code—one of her mother's this time—and jabbed the SEND command.

The pulse stopped. The light turned green.

"Authorization accepted." With an almost jaunty twirl, the drone ascended into the towers of crates, and disappeared.

Jesse let out a long breath. "If you're trying to show off, I can tell you right now, I'm well past impressed."

Ashe relaxed as well, though she tried not to show it. "I

was doing nothing of the sort. A slightly out-of-date code, that's all. I had it handled."

He gave her an amused, sideways glance. "Never thought otherwise."

Within a few minutes, the drone had retrieved four crates about the size of hay bales and deposited them on a hover-transport.

"Care to peek at the spoils?" Ashe bypassed the lock of the closest one. Inside lay a row of Seraphim scoped rifles in gunmetal gray, the Arbalest logo etched into their black stocks. "How do you like those, Jesse McCree?"

A fixed stare answered that question. With reverent intensity, he reached out, fingers brushing along a barrel. "I like them just fine."

"Top of the line," Ashe continued. "Intimidating, accurate, and complete with lethal and nonlethal modes. Exactly what we'll need."

"Robbing a corporation with their own guns," said Jesse. "It's almost poetic."

"I'm not interested in poetry." Ashe shut the crate again. "I'm interested in profit. C'mon, let's get back."

The tunnel felt shorter on the return trip, the hover-transport humming alongside them. Ashe felt as if she were floating, too, and she couldn't help but smile. They'd done it: step one in getting what she was owed, and in building a life of *her* choosing.

When they reached the end of the tunnel, they steered the hover-transport as close as they could to the cargo platform, then dragged the heavy crates onto it. Jesse hit the UP on the command display, and the platform began to rise, smooth as silk.

"Once we're topside," said Ashe, "B.O.B. can carry the crates to the truck. I've already used my parents' credentials to scrub these identification numbers from the cargo manifests and adjust the inventory levels. Poof, gone! It'll be like we were never—"

"Uh, Ashe?" Jesse pointed at crates. "Are those supposed to do that?"

"Huh?"

The inset displays on the crates had begun flashing—one message, over and over: *Warning! Warning!*

"Warning about *what*?" said Jesse.

"I'm not sure." Ashe furiously tapped the tablet, searching the crates' interface. "Give me a second."

Suddenly, the message changed.

Storage location proximity exceeded. Security ordnance activated.

"Security ordnance..." Jesse appeared over her shoulder. "Does that mean a *bomb*?"

"I–I don't . . ." Ashe swiped through screen after screen. "There must be some sort of explosive fail-safe on the containers to prevent theft."

"Can you turn it off? Hack it or something?"

"*Hack* it? I can't even *find* it!" The beeping picked up speed as Ashe hit every option she could see, but the warning continued to flash. "It must be accessible only from the warehouse."

Jesse paled a little, eyes going to the edge of the platform. Ashe saw what he was thinking, but even if they could drag all four crates to the edge in time, there wasn't enough room between the platform and the wall to push them over.

Jesse realized that, too. "We gotta make this platform go faster—"

"It only goes one speed, McCree!"

They locked gazes, and Ashe saw fear in his eyes. The same fear, she suspected, that he saw in hers. Then, in unison, they turned to the shaft running alongside the cargo platform, the rungs set in the wall. "How fast do you think you can climb?"

Jesse blinked. "Let's find out."

She dropped the tablet and bolted for the edge of the platform, boosting herself onto the rail.

"Wait!"

She turned back to see Jesse pulling the rifles from the case.

He tossed one to her. "Here!"

Ashe caught it, then slung the Seraphim's strap over her shoulder and jumped. For one heart-dropping moment, she was airborne, gravity's claws grabbing at her. Then her hand caught one rung and her foot, another. She wasted no time starting to climb. A grunt below told her that Jesse was close behind. Quickly, they outpaced the platform, but the beeping was getting faster and faster, echoing off the concrete walls.

"Ashe . . ." The tone of Jesse's voice told her what words didn't need to.

The opening of the shaft was getting closer and closer. But the cargo platform was still rising, and if the bombs in those crates went off, they would obliterate everything around *and* above them.

They were in the barrel of a gun, right before it was about to fire.

"B.O.B.! Help!"

Two meters from the top of the ladder, a scream of metal sounded, and a huge arm appeared. It grabbed Ashe, lifting her from the shaft like a toy and depositing her carefully on a floor now strewn with debris. Across the shed, the door was gone, a B.O.B.-sized hole in its place.

"McCree, too!" The order came out tinged with desperation. Below, the beeping had turned to a wail.

B.O.B.'s other arm plunged into the shaft, and a moment later, out came Jesse. But all around them, lights flashed, warning of the platform's imminent arrival. Ashe's blood drained into her boots. They were still too close, and even if they ran now, they'd never get clear in time.

It was too late.

Suddenly, B.O.B. clutched the both of them to his chest. The omnic shot to the other end of the shed and through the hole, taking two more hulking strides before falling to his knees and wrapping himself around her and Jesse. Ashe gasped, crushed within the metal embrace. But there was no time to fight.

A moment later the world lurched and a roar enveloped them, bringing with it a scorching heat. She would have screamed, if she'd been able. Instead, all Ashe could do was press her eyes closed and wait for it to be over.

Which was an eternity, compressed into the span of a few seconds.

Then B.O.B. loosened. Ashe pushed free of him, rolling onto the singed grass so that she was looking up at the butler. A bright glow of orange haloed him—the shed, engulfed in flames.

"Whoooo!" Jesse lay an arm length away, grinning madly. He let out a half laugh, half cough and turned to her. "Well, I've had my fill of excitement for the evening. You?"

Ashe ignored him and jumped to her feet. "B.O.B., are you okay?"

The omnic stood, creaking a little, and shook himself like a dog. But besides a few scorch marks, the butler seemed none worse for wear.

"We made it." Her voice shook as she said it. So did the rest of her, a little.

"Thanks to B.O.B.," said Jesse.

"Yeah, he's a great butler *and* bodyguard, when it comes down to it." Ashe shifted the strap on her shoulder, bringing the rifle around. "And we're not walking away empty-handed, either."

"Yup." Still on his back, Jesse gestured toward the warehouse complex. "Now all we gotta worry about is them."

Ashe turned. In the distance, a cluster of security drones were heading straight for them.

And they were closing in fast.

CHAPTER 5

From the frying pan into the fire.

"Get your butt up," Ashe yelled at Jesse. She slung the rifle over her shoulder and began to run.

As unconcerned as he'd sounded a moment ago, Jesse was on his feet in a flash. Followed by B.O.B., they bolted back up to the ridge. The boulders there gave them some cover, but not enough to fully hide their escape and, behind them, the lights of the security drones grew brighter.

The truck was where they'd left it, hidden near a thicket of desert sage.

"Drive!" Jesse started to climb into the truck's cargo bed. "I'll try to keep them off us."

Ashe pushed him aside. "You said revolver," she said. "*I said rifle*, remember? You drive; I shoot."

Jesse hesitated for a moment, but there was no time for an argument she'd end up winning anyway. "Shoulda grabbed some extra ammo, I guess."

"Live and learn." Ashe turned to her butler. "You hide, B.O.B.; those are Arbalest drones. They get one good look at you and our cover is blown. Once we're away, head for home on foot."

The omnic nodded and went dark, crouching in between the rocks.

Ashe jumped into the truck bed as Jesse revved the engine. A moment later, they were moving, but the terrain was bumpy enough to keep them from gaining much speed. Meanwhile, the security drones were drawing closer. B.O.B. wasn't the only one she couldn't risk them seeing. Ashe took a few precious moments to tear a bit of the lining from her duster, then wrapped it around the lower half of her face. It would have to do.

The desert opened up before them as they reached the old access road they'd come in on earlier. The moment the truck's tires hit the asphalt, Jesse floored it, and they began to fly.

But not fast enough.

The drones were in range now, half a dozen of them. They were silver and bulbous, almost beetle-like, each equipped with a glaring spotlight bright enough to make spots dance in front of Ashe's eyes.

"Desist your movement." The drones announced in unison, forceful and metallic. *"Please ready yourself for identification and investigation."*

Not a chance. Ashe raised the rifle. The truck rattled over the aging road, but she took a deep breath, steadying herself before she pulled the trigger.

BANG!

One of the lights exploded, quickly followed by a scrape of sparks as the metal carapace of the destroyed robot tumbled across the asphalt. Immediately, the remaining drones tightened their formation, front ones acting as a shield for the back.

Ashe let out a bark of laughter. "One down!"

"Only one?" Jesse called back.

"I'm workin' on it!" She raised the rifle again, but the truck dipped as it hit a pothole, tossing her like a toy. Sharp pain burst through her as she came down hard on one elbow. "Ah, damn it! You wanna drive straight, McCree?"

"I am!" Jesse called back. "You want a smooth ride? 'Borrow' a truck with lev rims next time!"

She ignored him, pulling herself up in time to see their pursuers approaching again, this time more aggressively.

"*Excessive aggressive force detected.*" Their spotlights flashed menacingly. "*Enabling defense protocols.*"

That didn't sound good. Ashe threw herself down, rolling to the tailgate as a hail of projectiles filled the air where she'd just been. They bounced off the truck's cab, a few of them rolling back to where she lay. Rubber shots, about the size of a clementine. Nonlethal . . . most of the time. These security drones weren't designed to kill, but they could incapacitate effectively. Next level of response would be tranquilizer darts. A couple of those and she'd be out like a light.

Which meant she had to work fast.

Ashe tightened her grip on the rifle and popped back up, letting loose a string of rapid fire, barely taking time to aim. Even so, two more of the drones went careening off into the desert.

A moment later, something whizzed past her ear. She didn't need to see it to know what it was. The security drones had escalated force, this time without warning. She ducked back down behind the tailgate again.

Three left. Ashe checked her remaining ammo. She could handle them . . . maybe.

But when she peeked out again, the remaining security drones had fallen back, and were now trailing the truck at a significant distance.

"Are they giving up?" Jesse called out. *"Do those things give up?"*

No, they don't. Ashe prickled with apprehension. So, if they were choosing to retreat, it could only mean—

Suddenly, lights burst to life in the sky in front of them, even more blinding than the drones' spotlights had been. Jesse hit the brakes without warning, throwing Ashe forward. But there was no time to be annoyed. More drones were in front of them, their black armor inky in the headlights of the truck.

"Attention! Cease your movement or we will cease it for you."

Ashe gritted her teeth. Great—the damn security drones had called for reinforcements.

There were only four of the newcomers, but they were bigger than the other drones, and more heavily armed. They descended until they were only a few meters in front of the truck, and hovered there. One look at their armor told her they'd be far harder targets to take down than the others.

"Hey, Ashe," said Jesse.

"Yeah?"

"You ready to give up?" He glanced back at her in the side mirror, a sly look in his eyes.

"Not a chance."

"Good." His gaze went forward again. "Then get down low and hold on tight."

Ashe crouched down and anchored herself as best she could while Jesse floored it. The truck shot forward, tires squealing. Then came the *crunch* of metal on metal, and one of the new drones flew over the cab of the truck. It crashed to the road behind them, lights flickering briefly before going dark. Meanwhile, the other drones scattered, only to regroup behind the fleeing vehicle. Ashe took aim and fired. Three shots, all aimed at the slight gaps between armor plates. It was enough to disable one of them, but two remained, and Jesse's gambit hadn't bought them much distance.

Suddenly, a panel opened up on one of the drones, and a barrel appeared. Ashe threw herself aside just in time, squeezing her eyes shut as a sound like a cannon firing filled the air. When she looked again, there was a hole where the back corner of the truck's cargo bed had been, the shredded metal still smoking slightly. She blinked at the carnage, stunned, as another drone fired, leaving a hole in the top of the truck. Luckily, it was on the passenger side. Otherwise, Jesse would have been left with one less head than he'd started the night with.

Ashe swore under her breath. At this rate, in another minute or two, there'd be nothing left of the truck . . . or them.

"Jesse!" she cried.

"I know, I know! I'm doing what I can; get back to shooting!"

She raised the rifle again, but as soon as she did, her stomach dropped like a rock. The first drone had its weapon primed again . . . and it was aimed squarely at Ashe.

She saw the barrel flash, what should have been the very last thing she saw in this life. But in the final instant, the truck swerved. The shot went wide, and Ashe went flying, tumbling along the bed of the truck and out the back before she could grab hold of anything. She lost her grip on the rifle as the world spun around her, coming to an abrupt—and painful—halt when she landed on her back alongside the road. For a long moment, the stars in the sky weren't the only ones she saw. Then she gasped, sitting straight up in the grass, her heart pounding so hard it felt twice its normal size.

Ashe winced. A lot of things hurt. But nothing felt broken.

The rifle . . . where was the rifle?

There.

It lay a few meters away. But the moment Ashe reached for it, the two drones appeared above her, blotting out the sky. She twisted, blinking away their glare, her vision clearing just in time to see the taillights of the truck disappearing around a bend in the road ahead.

But the drones ignored it, staying on her.

"Do not make any sudden movements," one ordered. *"Raise your hands. Slowly."*

Ashe obeyed, making sure they could see her empty

hands as she raised them above her head. Somehow, her mask had remained on, but her anonymity wasn't going to last for much longer.

And Jesse McCree was gone.

Should she have expected anything else? This night had gone truly, spectacularly wrong, and Ashe found she couldn't even blame him for running. Was he worried about what was going to happen to her? More likely, he'd weighed what would happen to *him* if he got arrested again and decided to take his chance at escape.

Ashe cursed. This should have gone better. *She* should have done better. And if a fight was enough for her parents to disown her, what were they going to do to her after *this* debacle?

"Stay where you are," a drone ordered. *"The police have been contacted and will be arriving shortly. As temporary authorized proxy, your rights are as follows: You have a right to counsel, if you can afford it. You have a right to medical attention, if you can afford it. You have a right to—"*

The drone exploded in a ball of fire as shots filled the air. Its remaining companion turned toward the gunfire, only to share the same fate a moment later. The security drone dropped like a rock at Ashe's feet. She kicked it away, and then jumped up and looked toward the road.

There was just enough light to make out the dark silhouette standing on the back of the truck, rifle raised.

"Move it, rich girl!" Jesse jumped down to the road. "There's more coming!"

Ashe looked behind her. Sure enough, lights dotted the sky in the distance, moving in on them fast, like a swarm of fireflies. She grabbed her rifle and bolted for the truck.

Jesse urged her along. He'd turned off the headlights and taillights, and was holding the passenger side door open for her. What was left of it, anyway.

Ashe jumped in, tense all over as Jesse made his way back around the cab and got them moving again. She stared at him as he drove, the determined look on his face accented by sharp lines of shadows.

"You . . ." She didn't know what to say. "You came back."

He looked at her askance. "You thought I'd leave you?"

"You could have gotten away."

"Well, sure." The stressed look was replaced by a smirk. "But that ain't my style. Took me a minute to notice you were gone. Anything broken . . . aside from your pride?"

"No, but I'm sure something will be if we don't get away from those drones." *Think.* There had to be a way out of this. "Hold on." Thankfully, the field glasses were still in her coat pocket. Raising them to her eyes, Ashe scanned the topographical mapping of the area. There had to be some way to escape, or at least a place to hide.

About a mile ahead, she spotted it.

"So," she said, "I've got a really bad idea."

"Oh, good." Jesse gripped the steering wheel tighter. "We've been playing it too safe so far."

She reached over and pressed the field glasses to his eyes briefly. "See it?"

"Uh-huh." He sounded tired. "That's a *really* bad idea."

"But it might work."

"Yeah," he said. "It might work."

There wasn't much confidence in his agreement. But they didn't really have a choice. The security drones were closing in. Wind whipping at her, Ashe kept an eye on them as Jesse steered through the dark night.

"'Bout to go off-road," he warned. "How close?"

"Close enough for them to see us," said Ashe. "Far enough for the plan . . . hopefully."

They'd have to cross their fingers the drones were using movement sensors, and not infrared.

The truck bounced as Jesse suddenly jerked the wheel to one side, turning them into the desert. Ashe looked forward again and adjusted the goggles. She'd have to time this just right.

"You see it?" said Jesse.

"Yes. Get ready." In the rearview mirror, she could see the drones as well.

They were committed now, caught in a vice that was about to snap shut.

"Almost there . . ." Ashe watched the topographical data rapidly update in her goggles. "Almost there, get ready—NOW!"

There was no time to wait and see what happened to Jesse. Ashe threw herself out the passenger side door of the truck, landing hard on the ground for the second time in the last quarter hour. This time, a thicket of sagebrush crunched beneath her, cushioning some of the blow. Still not an experience she wanted to make a habit of, though.

When she stopped rolling, it took all her willpower not to jump back up and look for Jesse. Instead, she stayed low as an explosion roared and a fireball lit up the sky, coming from the direction of the cliff that they'd driven the truck off of.

And none too soon. The drones appeared above her, obscured by the scattered brush. For a moment, they hovered, then continued toward the crash. Wasting no time, Ashe clutched her rifle and began to crawl in the opposite direction. She made it a dozen yards before she heard another rustle.

"Jesse?" she whispered.

"Here," he replied, just as quiet. "You think they bought it?"

"I think we need to be out of here before they get a chance to figure anything out."

Keeping as low and silent as they could, they made their way back to the road, and then disappeared into the night.

CHAPTER 6

"Wait, what?" Jesse looked at Ashe like she'd grown a second head. "You want to do *that* again?"

"Heck no." She finished with the last of her "adjustments" and then set the tablet down on her mother's desk, exhausted. It had taken a while, but she finally managed to adjust the reporting logs to recognize what had happened at the warehouse as an accident, the result of a retrieval drone's programming gone wrong. It hadn't meant to take the containers so far down the wrong tunnel, but it had, and they'd exploded. A freak accident. As to the guard drones, they'd pursued a pair of unidentified, but unrelated, trespassers. "Next time we're gonna get it right."

Dawn had passed, but it was still early, buttery morning sun streaming through the high windows of her parents' shared office. Ashe sat at one of the two desks, but Jesse relaxed on a couch, feet up on the coffee table as he worked through the breakfast B.O.B. had made for them. Ashe's food sat beside her, untouched, though she drained her coffee mug for the umpteenth time. B.O.B. immediately refilled it.

"All that havoc for a pair of rifles." Wrapped in a fluffy white robe that made him look a bit like a marshmallow, at least Jesse was clearly enjoying the manor life. "We almost didn't walk away from that, y'know?"

"Yes." Ashe gave him a pointed glance. "I was there."

"All those passwords and files of yours are something . . ." He paused and took a big bite of pancakes from the plate balanced precariously on his lap. Ashe fully expected the silk couch cushions beneath him to be drizzled with maple syrup any minute now. Almost dying certainly hadn't affected his appetite. "But they're not much good against secret bombs."

It had been a long, slow walk back to Lead Rose, at least until B.O.B. came back out to retrieve them with the family car. Jesse might have had a chance to clean up, but Ashe had set immediately to covering their tracks. And now, with dawn a few hours gone, Ashe felt every ache and bruise. Fatigue tugged at her eyelids, and she wanted nothing more than a very long soak in a very hot tub, but there was still work to be done.

"We got the rifles, didn't we?" It was enough to get started, though they'd have to buy some extra ammo.

"I'm not saying it wasn't a thrill." Jesse set his plate down—Ashe definitely saw a drizzle of syrup escape. "But we might not be so lucky next time."

She bristled. "We figured it out, though."

"What happens when we need to defuse another bomb? The two of us could be the best sharpshooters in the world, but when it comes to explosives, all that amounts to is a pile of very tiny pieces."

Ashe stood and put her hands on her hips. "Are you flaking on me, McCree?"

He gave her an unsure look. "You're good at planning, Ashe. But plans go awry."

"You're right." She nodded decisively. "We need more help."

"That's not what I meant—"

"A hacker," she continued, deep in thought. "And someone who knows munitions. Instead of worrying about bombs, we should be making them work for us. I have some ideas on that . . ."

"You have some ideas," Jesse said warily, "about blowing things up?"

"If the situation calls for it." All her fatigue was swept away in a tidal wave of considerations and strategies. They didn't just need to plan better, they needed to plan *bigger*. But Jesse still looked skeptical. "How much do you think that Seraphim rifle would bring you if you sold it?"

"Huh?"

"Enough so you wouldn't have to work on a farm for a few months at least. Well, if you want to bail, go. Take the gun and sell it." Ashe crossed her arms as she stood over him. "But if one rifle gets you a few months' worth of survival, think about how much ten rifles would get you? Or a case of power cells? Or an entire shipment of Arbalest's latest sniper scopes? You walk away now, McCree, and you'll be walking away from your chance at a fortune."

"There's more to life than money, Ashe."

"Sure," she said, "but it's easier to live life with it than without, right? Whatever you want, it's going to be a lot easier to get if you've got a full pocket."

She could see his doubt begin to waver. Still, Jesse thought for a long moment before replying. "Okay . . . so maybe we need more help."

Ashe suppressed a smile of triumph. "You sound like you might have a thought about that."

"I do," he said. "Julian."

"Your friend from the farm?"

Jesse nodded. "You know the reason he came out here? To try and work demolition on the transcontinental lines. He's been on his own even longer than me, and a lot of that in some of the worst spots of the Crisis. He picked up some . . . skills."

Ashe itched briefly at the thought of bringing on a near stranger, even if the idea had originally been hers. Jesse was one thing; she'd had a chance to size him up. But what did she know about this Julian? "He any good?"

Jesse shrugged. "Mostly."

"Mostly?"

"You'll understand when you meet him. And he's great at other things, too. Like getting his hands on things when you need them."

What kinds of things? Ashe wanted to ask, but left it alone for now. "Whatever he's good at, the most important thing is whether or not he can keep a secret. What makes you so sure we can trust him?"

Jesse turned thoughtful. "Because he's had my back. He was the one who talked the foreman into taking me on at Ace Valentine in the first place." His lips spread into a grin. "And he always saved me a spot in the chow line and made sure we didn't get the bunks with bedbugs."

It was Jesse's tone more than his words that convinced Ashe, but Julian wouldn't be enough. They needed someone who was better with computer systems than she was, and who could work quickly and in the moment. Someone with experience, and who was nearby.

Ashe went back to the desk and began inputting criteria into a custom search, starting with the local law enforcement reports. Dozens of files popped up as she picked at her breakfast, plenty of possibilities, but no one who jumped out at her as what she was looking for. Then . . .

"Well, this looks interesting," she said to no one in particular.

On the tablet was an almost empty file for a hacker named Frankie. No last name, and while their gender identity was confirmed as female, there were no pictures, and no physical description. She was suspected to have worked with the Diamondbacks—a local gang with a staggering bounty on their heads—as well as a number of other criminal enterprises. Lots of break-ins, including to a few Arbalest sites that Ashe had been fully sure were impregnable. Exactly the sort of person they needed.

Except there was no way to contact her.

Ashe thought for a moment. As much as she'd dabbled in the Arbalest systems, the world of elite hackers was one she had no place in. But she knew one important thing: that a hacker was more likely to find you than you were to find them.

Then something in the list of Frankie's suspected thefts caught her eye.

Okay, maybe she could work with that.

"So, this Julian," Ashe said to Jesse, now on his third stack of pancakes. "Do you know how to get in touch with him?"

Jesse laughed through a full mouthful. "Sure. Heck, I probably know where he is right now. Cutthroat Trout's."

"Excuse me? What under the sun is a—" It felt ridiculous to even say. "Cutthroat Trout's?"

"It's a hangout spot a little way outside of town."

"Never heard of it."

Jesse gave her an amused look. "You wouldn't have."

"Well, wherever it is, get a message to him to meet us there tomorrow night. I'll work on our hacker."

"Hacker?" said Jesse. "How are you going to do that?"

Ashe started tapping at the tablet again. "I'm gonna cast a little line into a big pond," she said, hitting the command to send the message she'd typed out. "And I've got a good feeling we'll get a nibble."

Cutthroat Trout's, as it turned out, was well beyond the outskirts of Bellerae, deep within a windy stretch of canyon that quickly set Ashe on edge. Especially after Jesse insisted they hide the car and walk the last mile. It was late enough that the sun was setting, staining the walls of the canyon around them a warm red. B.O.B.'s heavy tread trailed them as they walked, but even with him as an escort, Ashe found herself scanning every shadowed crevice they passed.

"How far is this place?" she said finally.

"Almost there," Jesse assured her.

As soon as he'd spoken, a low rumbling came. Ashe searched for the source as it rose around them, echoing off the stone.

Suddenly, B.O.B. grabbed her shoulder and pulled her back, right as a trio of hoverbikes sped by, kicking up a cloud of dust.

"See?" said Jesse as Ashe coughed.

She did, a minute later, as they rounded a bend and came out in front of the huge, gaping mouth of a cave.

A handful of people lingered outside of it, including the hoverbikes that had passed them. There were other vehicles as well, weathered trucks and a van with no back door. Jesse had been right to leave their town car behind; it would have stuck out like a panther in a pigsty here. No one looked at them as they approached, but Ashe was sure they were being watched, and closely. So she did the same, mentally cataloging who she saw. Cutthroat Trout's clientele seemed to be a mixture of drifters, punks, and gang members.

All in all, about as welcoming as a snakes' nest.

B.O.B. must have agreed, because he stopped Ashe again, keeping her from going any farther.

"Don't fuss," she snapped, shoving his hand off her. "You'll give us away." It was a bit jarring, looking at the omnic right now. Gone was his butler attire. It had been replaced with simple street clothes, and a jaunty little bowler hat that Ashe could have sworn made the omnic stand a bit straighter when they put it on his head. It was all part of their "disguise."

"You know, you're a tad too recognizable, Miss Elizabeth Caledonia whatever whatever," Jesse had said. "Not that I expect the folks at Cutthroat Trout's to spend a lot of time keeping up on the local elites, but plenty are from around Bellerae. And if you're spotted, there's going to be some questions."

So B.O.B. wasn't the only one who got a makeover. Ashe had traded her fine clothes for black pants and a short crimson coat, nearly the same shade as the wig she wore under a black cowboy hat. It was a tad dramatic, but Jesse swore she'd blend in. And Ashe found that when she'd looked at herself in the mirror, she saw someone else entirely.

And that hadn't bothered her one bit.

"Don't worry, big guy," Jesse said to B.O.B. "It looks

rough around the edges, but this here is a semi-legitimate business. They don't like trouble any more than we do."

Clearly, Ashe noted, as they entered the mouth of the cave. It was wide at the front, but tapered quickly into a corridor, a perfect kill zone for the gun turrets mounted around the ceiling. No one stopped them or filled them with lead as they proceeded to the rear. Ashe took that to mean that they were welcome. About fifty yards in, the tunnel widened again, and they came to a raised dais with a young woman sitting behind a rounded desk at its center flanked by a squad of bouncers, some of whom were nearly as big as B.O.B. She had dark hair and a tawny brown complexion stained neon pink from the vibrant hologlasses she wore.

"Jesse McCree," she chirped, without looking up from her tablet. "Welcome back! I heard about your trouble over at Ace Valentine's. My condolences, cutie."

"Thanks, Jaya." Jesse tipped his hat to her. "These are my friends. It's their first time here."

"Well, that's a treat! Hope you enjoy yourselves." Jaya nodded to direct them inside. "Julian is waiting for you."

Beyond the dais, the tunnel opened up abruptly, and Ashe had to suppress a sensation of vertigo as they entered a massive, dimly lit cavern, filled with a thick haze of smoke and a cacophony of laughter, shouting, and engines revving somewhere below. The floor of the cavern was a dizzying five stories straight down. Ashe, McCree, and B.O.B. stood at the top of a walkway that sloped down, leading to a large platform of stone in the center of the space.

On the platform were folks of every size, shape, gender, and hue—a more diverse gathering than Ashe had ever seen before. Half were wearing tech that even she would consider pricey. The rest looked like they might just as easily pick her pocket. But there was a sense of camaraderie as the patrons mixed indiscriminately, gathering around tables, laughing, and doing business. Except in one corner, where more bouncers were breaking up a fight that no one nearby seemed to care enough take notice of.

But what really hooked Ashe's attention was the cheering crowd pressed up against the rail enclosing the platform. A moment later she saw why: circling the base of the platform was Cutthroat Trout's own hovercycle track, a harrowing-looking loop filled with the sort of obstacles that *definitely* were not allowed in regulation races. As they descended the walkway, Ashe watched on a holoscreen as the current racers sped around the track, the two leaders barely a length apart as they approached the finish line. The second-place racer, unable to advance, swerved suddenly onto a narrow, curved ramp. Ashe sucked in a breath as they flew off the edge and through the air—only to land hard. The racer wobbled briefly before being thrown from the bike, which rolled a few times before coming to a defeated stop.

"And that's another win for the unstoppable Dezba!" Jaya's voice boomed through the cavern. "Tough luck to a hopeful Fee, who wiped out on everyone's favorite obstacle, the Neckbreaker! But nothing ventured, nothing gained. Maybe next time, buddy!"

"My whole life I've lived in Bellerae," Ashe said. "And I didn't know about this place."

"I don't think they usually cater to your type," Jesse quipped. He pointed across the room to a young man sitting alone at a table. "There's Julian."

"Jesse!" Julian's face lit up with a bright smile as they approached. He was shorter than Jesse, and slighter, with red hair and a thick spray of freckles across his face—except on the left side, which was shiny pink with scarring that ran over his cheek and down his neck into the threadbare work shirt he wore. "You're a sight for sore eyes. Thought the sheriff had run you right out of town until I got your message."

"Not yet." Jesse sat, as did Ashe, though B.O.B. remained standing. "These are the friends I told you about."

"Ah, yes, the mysterious unnamed friends." Julian held out a hand to Ashe. "Nice to meet you, miss—"

"'Unnamed friend' is fine for now," said Ashe, though she shook his hand.

Julian only smiled wider. "Well, you've got my attention, McCree. What's this about?"

"A job," said Jesse. "Well, *jobs*. But I'll let my friend here tell you more. She's the brains."

"You say that as if I'd ever think you held that role." Julian waved at a stray fly as he picked at the bar nuts on the table."

Jesse's face scrunched with revulsion. "Are you seriously eating those? They're probably older than you are."

"Hey, free food is free food." Julian popped another nut in his mouth. "So, let's hear it."

"Hang on for a few minutes," said Ashe. "I was hoping we might have one more person joining us."

Ashe scanned the strangers surrounding them. Any one of them could be Frankie. A bald woman covered in tattoos passed by, her gaze catching Ashe's for a moment. But she looked away quickly, not breaking stride. At another table, a young woman gazed intensely at a tablet, but when Ashe looked closer, she was running some sort of numbers, probabilities on the next race maybe.

Did Frankie get her message? If she did, would she show?

A fly crossed in front of Ashe's vision and she swatted at it automatically, barely missing the insect. But it wasn't deterred, circling once more before landing on the table. A moment later, a tiny holoscreen projected from it, showing a single word.

Hi.

Ashe looked closer. It wasn't a fly—it was a very small drone of some kind. She grinned. "Shy? We don't bite."

"Is that who we're waiting for?" said Julian, cracking a pistachio shell with his teeth.

"No," said a voice. "I think that would be me."

They all turned as a young woman approached the table. She looked about Ashe's age, dark-skinned and round-featured, with a sturdy build and short, twisted curls of lavender hair. The most noticeable thing about her was the hologlasses she wore—round and rimless, they were the most delicate pair Ashe had ever seen.

Ashe leaned back in her chair. "Frankie?"

The young woman nodded and took the last empty seat. As she sat, the tiny drone flew up and alighted on the edge of her hologlasses. "You got my attention."

"You did?" said Jesse. "How?"

It hadn't been that hard. "Sent her a message about where we'd be tonight," said Ashe. "Told her to come say hi."

Frankie nodded. "But only after a message that said 'Hey, Frankie, wanna make some real money? Just enter the password.'"

"Which was?" Julian leaned forward, riveted by the exchange.

"What she stole from an Arbalest shipment three months ago." Ashe smirked, recalling the report she'd seen in the Arbalest files. "What she *really* stole. Nicely done, by the way."

Frankie looked pleased. "Yeah, they really didn't want it leaked they lost those processor cores, huh? Why look incompetent when you can just cover it up?"

Ashe pointed. "Frankie, this is Jesse, and that's Julian."

"And that behemoth behind you?" said Frankie.

She was talking about B.O.B. "Just a big hunk of metal. Don't worry about him." This was the moment Ashe had been waiting for. "What I really want to talk to you about is money. Specifically, more money than you've ever seen before."

Julian's brow furrowed in confusion, but Frankie merely waited, hands calmly folded in front of her.

"A series of heists over the next few months," Ashe continued, "targeting weapons tech shipments. All planned by me, and all extremely profitable. Julian, I've heard you know explosives. And Frankie here can hack with the best of them. Jesse is a crack shot. And me?" She let the words hang for a moment. "I've got all the information we need to get filthy rich."

Frankie's expression didn't change, but a shade of greed passed across Julian's face.

"Hold on," said Jesse, eyes narrowed with suspicion. "I can vouch for Julian, but how do we know we can trust you, Frankie?" He turned to Ashe. "Didn't you say she's part of the Diamondbacks?"

At that, Frankie frowned. "I've *worked* with the Diamondbacks. I'm not one of them. I'm a freelancer; I do what I want, when I want. Or when I think the price is right. And if you want to talk about trust—Julian, wasn't it? Why don't you ask these two why they haven't told you what her name is. Her *real* name."

It was McCree's turn to be surprised. "You know?"

"Of course," said Frankie, not taking her eyes off Ashe. "Info about weapons-tech shipments? Not too hard to get that when your name is all over the files. Isn't that right, Elizabeth Caledonia Ashe?"

Julian choked on the mouthful of pistachios he'd just swallowed. "She's . . . who?"

"Shhhhh," said Jesse. "Keep it down. We're not advertising that part of the job, okay?"

Ashe remained unbothered. "I suspected you'd figure that much out. Yeah, that's me. Call me Ashe."

"I'll admit your involvement was what intrigued me enough to come out here," said Frankie. "Why does a rich girl like you need more money?"

"I don't have money," Ashe said. "My parents do." She sighed. "It's a long story—"

"Oh, I saw the newspaper," interjected Frankie. "Not hard to put the pieces together after that. So, you've got information. What else? Hitting corporate shipments isn't as easy as it sounds. What kind of equipment do you have?"

Ashe traded an unsure look with Jesse. "Well, we're still working on that."

"Look," said Frankie, "if you want my help, you're going to have to give me the rundown. What have you got?"

Ashe bit the inside of her lip. "Two rifles."

Frankie looked unamused. "That's it? No hoverbikes? No scanners or convoy traps?"

"They're *really* nice rifles," Jesse pressed.

"Yeah, that's it," said Ashe. "So far. We're working on it. But if that's all that's keeping you from saying yes, well, trust me—it's going to be your loss."

They all jumped as Julian slammed a hand down on the table. "Well, sounds like fun. I'm in!" He got to his feet, a distant look in his eyes. "And I have an idea."

And then he was gone, disappearing into the crowd surrounding them.

"You sure about him, McCree?" Ashe said to Jesse. "He seems—"

"Excitable," Frankie finished.

Jesse smiled. "He grows on you."

Ashe turned to Frankie. "What about you? You with us?"

Frankie considered the two of them for a minute. "We getting equal shares of the profits?"

"We are now," said Ashe. It was a lot of ground to give up, but without Frankie, her plans would be a heck of a lot harder. Anyone with half a lick of business sense would agree, this was a sound investment.

Another silent moment passed between them.

Then Frankie sighed. "Well, I've done stupider things in my time for the promise of less. I'm in, too."

"Fantastic. Welcome aboard." Ashe reached out a hand and they shook, right as Julian came loping back, smiling like a kid who'd found a secret stash of candy.

"Good news," he announced. "I've got a way to get us some hoverbikes."

Jesse grinned. "See, told you he was good at getting things you need."

Ashe remained unconvinced of that point. "Uh, how?"

"Next race," said Julian. "Dezba is racing again, and she hates how easy it's gotten to win lately. So, I made a wager with her. One of us wins against her, and she'll give us four bikes."

"That's it?" snorted Frankie. "Just beat an undefeated racer?"

"Wait," said Jesse. "A wager?" His face turned stony. "Julian, what did you bet? What does Dezba get if *she* wins?"

"Well." Julian rubbed the back of his neck with one hand. "I didn't have much money to wager with, so I bet Ashe's omnic."

CHAPTER 7

"**Y**ou did *what?*"

The only thing that kept Ashe from knocking out Julian's teeth was McCree. He jumped up when she did, putting himself between her and Julian. "Whoa, Ashe. Calm down."

Julian raised his hands defensively. "I thought we needed hoverbikes. This will get us hoverbikes. And you said he was just a big hunk of metal."

"Yeah, *my* hunk of metal." Ashe moved protectively in front of B.O.B. It was true he didn't act like most omnics, but he'd returned to her after the war and cared for her more than her parents ever had. Sure, she'd thought about what would happen to B.O.B. when she turned eighteen, but that was months away. To lose him right now... "B.O.B. isn't just some toy you can give away."

"Now, calm down," said Jesse. "No one is wagering B.O.B. Omnics can't be wagered these days, any more than a person can be."

"That may be true where folks follow the law," said Frankie, lights flickering across her hologlasses. "But here? Julian already locked in the bet. Try to bow out now, and B.O.B. goes to Dezba by right of forfeit."

Now Ashe was really gonna kill Julian. "Are you kidding me?"

Jesse frowned. "She's not. House rules."

"That's it. B.O.B., we're out of here—"

"You won't get far," said Frankie. "Laws might not be enforced in Cutthroat Trout's, but wagers are."

Ashe swore under her breath. "Well, how are we supposed to race without a bike?"

"Already taken care of," Julian said from behind the safety of Jesse. "I got us a house hoverbike. They lend them out to entice visitors to try their hand at racing, keep things fresh and exciting."

Ashe glared at him. "And you're gonna tell me some borrowed hoverbike is half as good as that Dezba's?"

"It doesn't need to be." Frankie smiled, gesturing for them to sit down again. She leaned in conspiratorially. "Those bikes can be hacked. I can make sure the only rider who crosses that finish line is ours."

Ashe narrowed her eyes. "You mean cheat?"

"Half the races here are as shady as they come," said Julian. "In Cutthroat Trout's, it's only cheating if you get caught."

"And we won't get caught," Frankie added. "I'm too good. In fact, consider this an audition."

If Frankie could do what she said she could . . . Ashe turned back to B.O.B. The omnic stood behind her loyally, emotionless. He wasn't some piece of tech. He was a person. Was she really willing to risk losing him for a— a bet?

Did she have a choice? It was her ideas that had led to this. *She* was the one with the plans, and the need to stick it to her parents. To do that, they needed equipment. Another Arbalest warehouse heist—unarmed, without wheels—was too risky. She and Jesse had been lucky to survive their first excursion. And while a hoverbike race wasn't the safest activity in the world, especially not on Cutthroat Trout's course, it was a heck of a lot less risky. They needed hoverbikes. And here was an opportunity to get them.

"Sounds like we're committed at this point," Ashe grumbled, not willing to give Julian the satisfaction of her full buy-in for his idea. "Okay. We'll do it."

"Can you ride?" Frankie said to Ashe.

"Wait," said Jesse. "That course is dangerous. She's the brains, remember? I'll do it. I'll race."

"The hell you will, McCree." Ashe flashed him a look that made him sit back in his chair. "I've ridden a hoverbike before. I know what I'm doing." She left out the part where she'd crashed it, damaging it to the point that her parents refused to have it fixed. "And there's no way I'm putting B.O.B.'s fate in anyone else's hands. If anyone is going to lose him, it's gonna be me. You got me?"

He nodded carefully.

"Then it's settled." Frankie blinked a few times as her glasses flashed. The miniature drone perched on them lifted off again, zipping over to Ashe's ear, where it latched on gently to her lobe. "This will let me communicate with you during the race."

"And then what?" said Ashe.

"And then you do your damn best to stay upright on that obstacle course"—Frankie grinned—"and let me do the rest."

As the hacker pulled out a tablet and got to work, Ashe turned to B.O.B. "Don't worry," she said quietly to the omnic.

"Win or lose, if anyone tries to take you, they're going to have to get through me."

To this day, Ashe wasn't sure what had happened. Maybe she'd taken the turn too fast, maybe she'd clipped the edge of the stone wall. One moment she'd been buzzing around the estate, scaring the groundhogs, and the next . . . She remembered getting back up, both hands scraped and one knee dripping blood. The hoverbike was in even worse shape.

Her parents had been overjoyed. They'd hated the vehicle; it was "dangerous" and "unladylike." Ashe had only agreed with one of those assessments; after all, wasn't the danger part of the appeal?

But Cutthroat Trout's racetrack was nothing like the grounds of Lead Rose, and the view from the track was very different from the one above it. The track hadn't looked so big from up high, and there was something distinctly more menacing about the obstacles, now that she knew she'd have to navigate through them. Mud pits and ditches, hidden pipes that spit flames or projectiles . . .

Beneath Ashe, the hovercycle hummed, as if it couldn't wait for the race to get started. She didn't quite agree. It was hard to believe that people did this for fun. Then again, the prize purses for the races were pretty good. Maybe, for some people, a few minutes of adrenaline-fueled, high-speed danger was more appealing than endless back-breaking labor in a factory or on a farm.

The starting line was the same as the finish line, and from where she waited, she could see the Neckbreaker, that thin swirl of ramp that had earned itself such a charming moniker. From this vantage, Ashe had a better appreciation of the dense cluster of obstacles surrounding it, which would force even an experienced hovercycle rider to slow some. But taking the ramp gave the racer a straight shot, though there was the little matter of the inevitable jump at the end. One that most riders failed to land . . . one that some people even failed to walk away from. The divot scraped into the earth by the earlier, ill-fated racer was still apparent. They, at least, had survived to race another day.

Ashe gripped the handlebars of the hovercycle and revved the engine. Forget about any death-defying jumps, she'd be lucky if her loaner bike managed to make it to the end of the race intact. It was an old model, even older than the hovercycle Ashe used to have, cobbled together from an antiquated chopper-style motorcycle body and some middling lev rims. Granted, it had some style—all chrome and sleek steel, as opposed to the other racers' bikes, which were neat and curvy with their industrial plastics. Hopefully, it was also fast and sturdy enough to give Frankie time to do whatever she needed to. In the meantime, it was up to Ashe to stay in the race.

Inwardly, she allowed herself a laugh. If only her parents could see her now. But that humor dissipated quickly. There was too much to lose, too many ways for this to go wrong.

No . . . she couldn't think like that. She needed to ride well, and trust that Frankie would work her magic.

Another bike glided over to Ashe. She could feel the stare of the rider, even behind the tinted shield of their helmet.

"So you're the one I'm about to win myself a new omnic from." Removing her helmet, Dezba turned out to be a middle-aged woman, with an unruly shock of graying black hair and a warm tan complexion. Her cheeks were peppered with tattoos—tiny vertical lines that were strangely imposing.

Ashe sat a little straighter on the hovercycle. "And you're the one I'm gonna get a set of new bikes from." It wasn't hard to sound confident. At least, it was easier than feeling it. Dezba was a much more experienced rider, and they both knew it.

The woman laughed—a deep, throaty sound. "Keep dreaming, kid." She pointed to the tattoos. "Like 'em? One for every omnic I took down during the war. They're dangerous, y'know."

Ashe felt her cheeks flush with anger. "B.O.B. ain't like that. He's—"

"Good?" said Dezba. "So were the other omnics. Until they weren't. But don't worry. I'll be selling yours once I win this race. Big guy like that? He's worth a small fortune to the right folks."

Ashe's stomach clenched, but before she could say anything else, a young woman with brown hair and freckles approached them.

Dezba nodded. "Alyssa."

"Hey, Dezba. Nice racing tonight. But try not to win too quick this time, 'k?" She turned to Ashe. "Can I get your name? For the bookies."

"Uh . . ." Her real name was no good; she needed a cover. Her mother's voice popped into her head, from when Ashe had crashed her hoverbike. What had she called it? A . . . a . . . "Calamity," she remembered finally. "Name's Calamity."

"Thanks. And good luck," said Alyssa, before departing. "You'll need it!"

Dezba shot her a confident smirk. "See you at the finish line, Calamity." She turned. "Or not."

Ashe winced. She took a deep, steadying breath before putting on her own helmet and steering the bike to where the other racers were lining up. There were a total of six in this race, including Ashe. Only five opponents she had to beat.

She could do it. She *had* to do it.

"Are y'all ready for another race?" Jaya's voice rang out, to the cheers of Cutthroat Trout's patrons.

"Are *you* ready?" This voice was Frankie's, piped directly into Ashe's ear.

"Hope so," Ashe muttered, and got ready.

Hovering above the track, the red race lights began to count down. Red. Ashe revved the engine . . . Yellow. She pressed her heels into the metal rests . . .

GO!

The moment the green lights appeared, Ashe squeezed the accelerator. The bike surged forward, startling her enough that she wavered a little and was forced to slow and regain control, losing valuable ground. *Beginner's mistake*, she chided herself, focusing her attention on what lay ahead.

The bike, as it turned out, was fast. She shot forward, settling in the middle of the pack as they pulled away from the starting line. But the vehicle wasn't going to be much competition for the other racers' bikes; that much she could tell immediately. So, if she wasn't going to have any advantages with speed, Ashe would have to rely on skill.

Ashe passed a racer on the right, barely skirting a firetrap, which spit out red-and-yellow flames a split second after she passed it. That put her in third place. Not good enough. Dezba was in second, behind a racer on an absurdly striped orange-and-yellow bike with a smiley face painted on the back. Ashe tried not to be distracted by Dezba, who clearly knew the course, weaving easily between the obstacles and then jumping a pit. She almost made it look easy.

Another racer came up beside Ashe and swerved toward her suddenly. Attention still on Dezba, Ashe jerked away from them, then overcorrected, nearly resulting in a collision with a cement wall.

"Hey, pay attention!" ordered Frankie. "This isn't going to work if you crash before I can do anything."

"Well, what are you waiting for?" Ashe ducked as a projectile fired at her from the wall of the cavern.

Frankie made a snorting sound that might have been a laugh. "You just watch what happens to Smiley Face there."

They'd almost completed the first lap. Dezba was making advances on Smiley Face, but they were half-hearted, as if she knew she still had plenty of time to take the lead. Then, suddenly, Smiley Face began to slow. From Ashe's vantage, she could see the rider hit the throttle, but the engine was making a strange noise, as if choking.

"Oh no," said Frankie dramatically. "Sounds like someone's power flow isn't routing correctly. What bad luck."

Bad luck, indeed. As Ashe watched, Dezba took the opportunity to speed up, coming around on Smiley Face's left side. The move was subtle, but effective. Dezba kicked one leg out, hardly a tap, but the move unbalanced Smiley Face, who veered abruptly, colliding with a pile of hay bales.

Smiley Face was out.

"One rider down!" Jaya's voice came again, above the distant sounds of excitement. Apparently, the crowd liked a little tragedy with their action.

"Okay, I'm impressed," said Ashe.

"You should be." No humility on Frankie's part. "If it's got a computer on board, I can hack it."

"Then do it ag—"

Ashe inhaled sharply as two more racers came up on either side of her. Almost close enough to touch, there was little room to maneuver as one feinted toward her with their bike. Ashe moved away, only for the other to repeat the movement. Barely righting herself in time, Ashe steered down the center of the pair, trying to get ahead of them. But they wouldn't let her.

"Frankie?" she cried.

"I need a second," snapped the hacker. "Julian says it's a team-up—two racers working together to take down an opponent. They're gonna try to take you out of the race."

"Yeah, I figured that part out already." Ashe dodged

another feint. She got a brief reprieve when one racer had to move out of the way of a mud pit, widening the space between them. "Can you do anything about it?"

"Uh . . ." There was silence for a moment.

"Frankie—" Desperation leaked into Ashe's voice.

Ahead waited the Neckbreaker. Its widest point was the base of the ramp, spreading across the middle of the track in a way that forced riders to go around it. Except the racers flanking Ashe clearly had no intention of allowing her to do so. They were forcing her onto the Neckbreaker. A glance in her rearview mirror compounded the problem: The last racer was only a couple lengths behind her, no doubt seeing what was up and taking advantage of the situation. If Ashe hit the brakes, she'd likely hit them, or at least spin out.

"Ashe," Frankie cried suddenly. "I need you to trust me. When I say steer left, you steer left!"

"What are you going to—"

"NOW!"

At Frankie's bark, Ashe veered her hovercycle to the left. The distance between her and the racer on that side closed sickeningly, but just as Ashe was about to hit them, their hovercycle jerked to the left, too. They cleared the Neckbreaker's ramp. But unlike Ashe, who corrected her path following that, the other racer kept turning. On the other side of Ashe, the second racer who had boxed her in was having the same problem. Ashe blew past them as they scraped along the exterior walls of the track, and then went down.

"Ooooh, more bad luck for our racers," announced Jaya, sounding more excited than sympathetic. "They're back on their feet, but there's no way they'll make up that lost ground."

"Locked their steering," said Frankie's voice in her ear. "They had to swerve. I made sure they couldn't unswerve."

Three down, two to go. Ashe smiled. The odds were moving in her favor. She accelerated as the rider in last place, who'd backed off a little, began to creep closer again. Their gain was slow, but it was a distraction at a point where Ashe needed all of her focus. Dezba was in the lead, and they were running out of laps.

As they passed the starting line for the second time, the last place rider made their move, accelerating as Ashe slowed briefly to avoid a ditch in the track. It was a smart move, calculated so that either Ashe had to steer into the obstacle, or let the rider pass by. Having no choice, she slowed her speed further, gritting her teeth with frustration as the rider came up on her right . . . and then promptly disappeared.

Jaya made a little bark of surprise. "Oh, what a waste of fine riding!" she said. "Someone wasn't watching for projectiles, shame, shame."

Ashe let out a breath. "Frankie, was that you?"

"Nope, that one was pure luck. But I wouldn't count on much more of that."

Ashe gripped the accelerator. It was down to her and Dezba, and there was no way the experienced rider was going to be taken down by something so mundane as a projectile.

But though Ashe squeezed every last bit of power she could out of the hovercycle, Dezba remained stubbornly ahead of her as they looped the track again.

Last lap. Time was running out.

For Ashe and for B.O.B.

"Two riders left, folks." Jaya's announcement punctuated Ashe's thoughts, making her tighten with stress. "One of our seasoned favorites, Dezba, versus the newcomer, Calamity. And as much as I love an underdog, the odds seem pretty certain about who is going to come out victorious."

"Want me to tell you the odds?" said Frankie.

"No!" spat Ashe. "Do something about Dezba."

"Relax, I'm just about to . . . Hm . . . Uh-oh."

"Uh-oh? What does 'uh-oh' mean?"

"It means we have a problem," said Frankie. "Remember how I said I could hack anything with a computer? Well, Dezba's bike seems to be more . . . analog than I expected. It doesn't seem to have one. At least, not one that controls any system that's gonna do you any good."

"So what you're saying is—"

"You're on your own, Ashe."

Great. There was no way her bike was going to overcome Dezba. Not with less than a lap to go. Which only left one option: the Neckbreaker.

Ashe tightened her grip on the hoverbike's handles. They needed those hoverbikes. But it wasn't the promised vehicles Ashe found herself fixating on. It was B.O.B.

She'd almost lost him once to the Crisis. She wouldn't lose him again. Not now, not like this.

So when Dezba blew past the ramp to the Neckbreaker, Ashe steered directly onto it, willing her bike to go as fast as it possibly could. The path narrowed almost immediately, becoming barely wide enough for the vehicle to navigate it. Which made it impossible for Ashe to peek and see where Dezba was below. This was a leap of faith, a last-ditch effort to get out in front of—

Something collided with Ashe, hitting her shoulder like a

punch. There was no time to feel pain; the bike tilted, giving Ashe a nauseating view of the track below, far enough down that her blood turned cold. She wrenched the bike back, nearly teetering in the other direction before righting herself.

It was a projectile. The spot where it had hit her stung like hell, making Ashe's whole arm tingle and tighten but, by some miracle, she kept control.

And barely in time.

The edge of the jump was coming up. Heart pounding and vision narrowing, Ashe kicked the fear out of her mind, along with B.O.B., Frankie's voice in her ear, Dezba, and all other distractions. There was only the track, the open air, and the ground below.

Nothing was going to stop her now.

The bike flew off the edge of the jump. Exhilaration filled Ashe as she careened forward and then began to fall. Steady . . . steady . . .

And then Dezba was right below her. Too close. Far too close.

Ashe kept her grip on the bike. She wasn't going to waver now.

But neither was Dezba.

Ashe landed with a jolt, clearing Dezba by inches. Stunned, her last opponent jerked her bike to one side, freeing Ashe to close the distance between her and the finish line. She sped across it, but something was wrong. The way the bike had landed . . . Something felt loose . . .

The concrete pillar came up too quickly for her to turn, and Ashe clipped the edge of it. The collision sent her into a spin, headed for the wall of the cavern. There was no time to right it.

So, she didn't try. With one last thought of how undignified it was to win the race this way, Ashe released the handlebars and tumbled from the bike, giving herself over to the unreliable ally that was luck.

CHAPTER 8

A she was hurt, and badly. What else would explain the all-encompassing roar that continued to surround her, even after the world stopped moving? She blinked at the blinding lights, certain they, too, were a sign of grievous injury, until a hulking mass appeared above her, blocking them out.

B.O.B.

He prodded Ashe briefly before gingerly picking her up and setting her on her feet.

It was then that Ashe realized the roar wasn't in her head.

It was applause.

And she was okay. Better than that, she'd won. Ashe had

crossed the finish line before the hoverbike gave out, and while her collection of scrapes and bruises was growing, the chopper had borne the worst of the damage. It lay a dozen meters away, mangled from its collision with the cavern wall and smoking faintly.

"How exciting was that finish, folks?" Jaya's voice rang out with genuine excitement. "Everyone give a cheer for our first-time racer, and now first-time winner, Calamity!"

The audience's approval rose again, turning thunderous.

"I'm fine." Ashe pushed B.O.B., who was still fussing over her, away. But there was no edge to her voice, only relief. She'd won. B.O.B. wasn't going anywhere. She looked up at the omnic with as much dignity as she could muster in the moment. "Don't say I never did anything for you."

B.O.B. blinked silently at her.

"That. Was. Unbelievable!" Julian's voice cut through the frenzied cries of the onlookers. He appeared on the track, followed by Jesse and Frankie. "The way you landed . . . and then how you sped across the finish line before you spun out and . . . BOOM!"

"Sure," she said wryly, stretching the tenseness from her muscles. "Nothing to it."

Jesse put a hand on her shoulder, briefly. "Glad to see you walking away from that. Wasn't sure it would happen for a second there."

Ashe tipped her head up at him and smiled. "Aw, were you worried about me, McCree?"

It might have been the lighting, but Ashe swore she saw a touch of blush in his cheeks.

"Well," he said quickly, "the whole 'let's get rich' scheme is dead in the water without you. Course I wanted you to make it out in one piece."

"Looked like you had everything handled to me," said Frankie, in an offhand manner, as if she didn't know exactly how the race had played out.

"Must've had a guardian angel," said Ashe. "An extremely talented one."

"Geez, if you can ride like that"—Julian's smile was ear to ear—"we're going to have no problem taking down the—"

Ashe jabbed a finger in his face, cutting him off. "Let's get something straight." Her prior serenity dissipated. "B.O.B. is a member of this crew, not something you can *wager*. And *I* make the plans for this team. You ever do something like that again, you're gonna wish you'd never come within a hundred miles of Bellerae. Understand?"

All the joviality disappeared from Julian's face. He nodded solemnly. "Yes, boss. I understand."

Ashe straightened. *Boss.* She liked the sound of that.

"Then I guess I better apologize again," he continued, a little sheepish.

Ashe glared at him. "Why?"

"It's only that . . . Well, it sounded like we could use some seed money. So I placed another bet." His eyes met hers, hopeful. "On you."

Ashe gaped, unsure what to say.

"You want to hear the odds now?" said Frankie.

Jesse gave her a knowing smile. "Because they were bad. And when you won, well . . . let's just say we're going to be able to upgrade those bikes right away."

Slight amusement crept onto Julian's lips as he waited for her to respond.

After a moment, Ashe sighed. "All's well that ends well, I suppose. I'm gonna have trouble staying mad at you, aren't I?"

"Most folks figure out how useful I am eventually," quipped Julian. "And once we add your race winnings into mine, well, it's a start."

"Unless I'm going to have to pay for that mess." She hooked a thumb at the ruined hovercycle Cutthroat Trout's had lent her.

"Nah," Julian said. "Happens all the time. Covered by the house."

"Hey, Calamity."

Ashe turned to find Dezba standing nearby, helmet off, and looking far less irritated than Ashe might have expected.

"Congratulations." The racer crossed her arms tartly. "Not sure how you pulled that win off"—the way her eyes flickered toward the others said she might have suspicions—"but you took on the Neckbreaker like a pro. I'll have your bikes waiting out front for you when you leave."

Ashe nodded. "Thanks."

"Rematch sometime?"

The smart answer would have been to say no, and never set foot on Cutthroat Trout's death trap of a racing course again. But Ashe couldn't deny the exhilaration the race had left her with. "Yeah, sure. One of these days."

"Great." Dezba gave her a quick wave and headed off the track. "See ya around, kid."

As the racer walked away, Alyssa approached again.

"Congratulations," she said with genuine admiration, holding out her tablet. "If you could please provide a valid account number, your winnings will be transferred to you."

"B.O.B.," said Ashe. "Take care of this." She turned back toward the others, catching sight of the hoverbike once more. "Actually, hold on. Are y'all going to rebuild that bike?"

"That old thing?" Alyssa shook her head. "Nah, it's headed for the trash pile. We've got plenty more where that came from."

"Hmm." Ashe was still eyeing the wreckage as B.O.B. finished the transaction.

"You got a look in your eye," said Jesse, nudging her with an elbow. "Whatcha thinking?"

"Not sure yet," said Ashe. "But I know one thing: We should spend some of those winnings on a good time tonight. How's that sound, crew?"

Julian through up his arms in triumph. "Woo! Sounds like a plan to me. They make the best loaded cheese fries here—burnt to a crisp, smothered in grease."

Frankie shrugged. "Yeah, I could eat some cheese fries. None of those bacon bits on mine, though. I'm a vegetarian."

Julian's mouth dropped open. "You know a pig would eat you if given the chance."

Frankie rolled her eyes.

"No, he's got a point," said Jesse.

"Seriously," Julian continued, "let me tell you about this one time, when I was working at a pork-processing plant . . ."

Ashe hung back as they headed topside again. Nodding at B.O.B., she gestured to the wreckage of chopper hovercycle. "Grab that before we leave, would you? You know what they say, one person's trash . . ."

"I'm gonna be honest," said Julian. "When Frankie dropped who you were, I expected you to live in a slightly nicer place."

"You don't like it?" Ashe played along as she threw open a set of shutters on the old barn that sat on the edge of Lead Rose's grounds. It wasn't much, but it was a wide-open space with plenty of room to work—once they cleared out the dust and old hay, Ashe figured. More importantly, it was private, in a place where they wouldn't encounter any prying eyes. "And here I was going to give you a nice spot to sleep in the loft, in the corner without the leak."

Frankie laughed as she set up a pile of equipment on an old worktable. "Fine with me. I've operated out of worse places."

"Me too," said Jesse. "But . . . we're not really going to start sleeping here, right?"

"No, McCree, you don't have to give up your nice featherbed and private bathroom," said Ashe. "But this is where we are going to keep anything related to our plans. No one has been out here in ages, it can't be seen from the main part of the estate, and there's a private road that accesses it. Perfect for staging our setup."

The four hoverbikes they'd won from Dezba sat in the center of the space. They'd spent the whole night at Cutthroat Trout's, and now the morning sun glinted off the bikes as it streamed through the open barn doors. They weren't the worst bikes Ashe had ever seen, but they definitely weren't the best, either. Better power cells were needed, to start, and the lev rims needed serious recalibration. And they could all use a fresh coat of paint. But getting them ready seemed like the best kind of challenge. Frankie had already begun work on hers, tearing out its electronic guts and strewing them across the dusty concrete floor.

Beyond the quartet of functioning bikes, B.O.B. had deposited the wreck of the chopper in a corner. There was something in it worth bringing out, Ashe knew, but exactly what was still taking form in her mind.

"Speaking of heists," said Julian, "when do we start?"

Now *that* was something Ashe was sure of. "Gonna be soon."

Frankie looked up from her work. "How soon? I've got a ton to do here. I can hold off on any major reworking of your bikes, but mine will need a full systems upgrade, and then some."

"How quickly can you do it?" said Ashe.

"Well, we're going to need to do some shopping, but . . ." Frankie thought for a moment. "Four days."

"You have three." Ashe brought up some documents on her tablet and set it to project so the others could see. A map appeared, showing a highlighted route. "First job should be a piece of cake. Arbalest is doing an automated transport of the schematics for new rifle scopes from one of its satellite locations to a local factory, in order to avoid any online piracy. Drones only, no humans or omnics involved.

Since it's the plans and not the actual product, they won't be expecting the local gangs to try and steal it, but there are plenty of folks on the virtual black market who would pay nicely for them." She pointed to a highlighted stretch of the map. "This is where we are going to hit the convoy. It's the middle of nowhere, right before they get to the Brisco Tunnel. Any time after that and we'll be too close to Bellerae. Not to mention we don't want to get boxed in inside a long stone tube." Ashe felt a rush of excitement. "I'll go over the rest of the details as we get the bikes ready."

But Jesse crossed his arms, looking skeptical. "You sure we're up for this, Ashe? Maybe we should, I don't know, practice a little? After last time—"

Julian perked up. "Last time? What happened last time?"

Ashe glared at Jesse. "LAST TIME we didn't have the kind of skills you and Frankie have. But we do now. I have a plan, one we're going to go over and over and over again until we can say it in our sleep. That's all the practice we'll need." She paused. "But if anyone has any reservations, if you don't want a chance at the kind of money that will ensure you'll never have to see the inside of a barn or a workhouse or a processing plant again, now's the time to walk away."

Ashe looked around the room, waiting. But everyone stayed right where they were.

"Okay, then," she said. "Let's go shopping."

CHAPTER 9

Unlike Cutthroat Trout's, Ashe *had* heard of Fort Starr. Nestled in the hills beyond the outskirts of Bellerae, the town dated all the way back to Caledonia's time, built up around the old fort that gave the place its name. Small and remote, with only a hundred or so residents, it had been mostly known as a tourist destination until the Omnic war broke out. Then it had turned into a waystation of sorts, a place for persons displaced by the fighting to rest for a few days, or to barter for supplies. Some of those folks never left, and the quiet little town became known for a particular brand of trade; it wasn't a black market exactly, but it also wasn't the sort of place respectable citizens did their shopping. But it *was* the sort of place that had the parts needed to whip the hoverbikes into shape, along with the other heist supplies they needed.

Once again, Ashe donned the Calamity disguise she'd worn to Cutthroat Trout's, brushing stray strands of the red wig away from her face as they drove into town. Its main street ran straight, ending at the eponymous fort, whose adobe walls were sun-baked and half crumbled. Lining the road were a variety of storefronts, many with hand-painted signs and windows advertising everything from hot breakfasts to military surplus. Jesse parked their latest "borrowed" truck (with lev rims this time) in front of a saloon that appeared to be doing a brisk trade, given the number of hovercycles parked out in front of it.

Climbing out of the vehicle, Ashe took a long look around and relaxed. They'd left B.O.B. at the mansion for fear he might be recognized, but there were enough people around that no one would pay close attention to the four of them. And Frankie had assured her that the residents of Fort Starr had a reputation for minding their own business.

"Hm," said Jesse, gazing around, "where to first?"

"We've got a list," said Ashe. "So let's start at the top." A nearby shop caught Ashe's eye and she pointed. "Ammo. We're going to need plenty of that for sure."

As they entered, a bell over the door tinkled, rousing the man dozing behind the counter. He sat up, skepticism growing in his face as he looked over the four of them. "Can I help you?"

"You sure can." Ashe ignored his dismissive tone as she scanned the shelves, filled with bullets of every caliber and style imaginable. "These." She grabbed a few boxes. "And these."

Box by box, she built a pile on the counter. By the time she was finished, the proprietor's reluctance had been replaced with eagerness, eyes bright at the prospect of a good sale.

"How much?" Ashe said. When he gave her the price, she nodded. "Frankie, pay the man."

"Hold on." Julian pushed his way in front of Ashe, an unamused look on his face. "This gentleman must be joking with you, because if he isn't, that's highway robbery."

The proprietor looked offended. "I assure you, my prices are always fair."

"Fair would be *half* of what you just quoted," said Julian. "And I bet that's exactly what we'll pay if we take our business down the street to one of your competitors. Hell, maybe even less."

"Not true. And you'd be getting inferior goods any-where else." But the proprietor's expression softened. "A discerning buyer like yourself wouldn't want that. I'm sure we can work something out." He gave another price.

Julian began to speak again, then stopped, and turned expectantly to Ashe. It took a moment for her to realize what he was looking for from her: approval. She felt a strange mix of annoyance and embarrassment. Sure, Julian had jumped in to negotiate with the ammo dealer without her permission, but he'd also stopped her from paying way more than what the bullets were worth. And now he was looking for her authorization before continuing negotiations.

As calculating as Ashe could be, haggling wasn't something she'd had much experience with. Maybe Julian *was* as useful as he seemed to think, after all.

Ashe kept her face neutral as she nodded. "Julian, why don't you and Jesse handle this while Frankie and I work on getting what we need for the bikes."

Julian smiled. "Sure thing, boss."

Ashe tossed a look at Jesse that said *Keep an eye on him*—useful or not, Julian could clearly be impulsive—then followed Frankie back outside.

The hacker had a little smile on her face as she scrolled through a list on her tablet. "First Cutthroat Trout's and now Fort Starr. Not your usual scene, huh?"

No. But she'd learn. "You say that like you come here a lot."

"Sure," said Frankie. "Plenty of times. I never know what kind of techy tidbits I'll find here. C'mon, I know someone who should have all the parts we need."

They made their way to the other end of the main street, passing store after store. Ashe saw canned food and military rations in their windows, clothing and travel gear, and, of course, plenty of weapons. She spotted a few Arbalest models here and there, but old ones, and most of which had seen better days. Clearly Fort Starr had a lot to offer, but that didn't mean all of it was good quality.

Frankie moved with familiar confidence, leading Ashe down a side street to a small warehouse with nothing but an old mud flap scrawled with the word OPEN hanging outside to indicate it was a place of business. Inside, Ashe was hit was an almost-immediate sense of claustrophobia. The space was brimming with engines, wheels, lev rims, and all other manner of vehicle parts, piled floor to ceiling. The only open area was off to one side, where an old woman sat, feet up on a desk, nursing a mug of steaming coffee. Seeing them, her face lit up.

"Frankie! Been a while." She was eighty if she was a day, Ashe judged, with snow-white hair that contrasted with her dark, wrinkled skin. But her eyes were bright and her smile sparkled—literally. Her two front teeth were plated with chrome. She put down the mug and stood as they came over, moving with surprising spryness. "You bring me anything good today?"

"Sorry, Mary. Today I'm buying, not selling." Frankie turned to Ashe. "Calamity, this is Metal Mary."

"Nice to meet you, ma'am." Ashe nodded politely.

"If you're looking for a part for a car, truck, or bike," Frankie continued, "she's the one to come to in Fort Starr."

"That's the truth," said Mary, her silver hoop earrings glinting in the cool light of the warehouse. "You need it, I got it. What'cha looking for today, young ladies?"

Mary's head wagged as Frankie scrolled through her list, only stopping once or twice with a question. The hacker had things well in hand, so Ashe perused the maze of piles as she waited, trying to discern a pattern to the haphazardly gathered collection of parts, but finding none. Mary seemed to know where everything was, though, pointing at things confidently as she consulted with Frankie.

A splash of color drew Ashe's attention—an old motorcycle gas tank balanced on a pile of mufflers. It had the glossy, bright-red sheen of a candy apple, and the remains of what looked like a pair of white wings on it. She went over and picked it up, turning it over in her hands. It wasn't what they were looking for, and wouldn't fit any of the bikes they had, but she liked it. She couldn't have said why, exactly, but she did.

"All set," said Frankie, appearing beside Ashe. "Mary is going to pull what we need, but it will take a little while. We might as well keep shopping while we wait."

Leaving Metal Mary's behind, they made their way back to the main street.

"What's next?" said Ashe.

"I need a new processor for the rig I'm building into my bike," Frankie replied. "And then there's some tools we should get if Jesse and Julian haven't . . . picked them up . . ."

The hacker trailed off, her gaze locking on something over Ashe's shoulder.

"Heeeey, Frankie," said a voice, with an edged sort of friendliness.

Ashe turned to find a pair of young men standing nearby— gang members, given the matching insignias they wore on their jackets. She tensed, recognizing the snake symbol. Not just gang members.

Diamondbacks.

"Look, Bez," the one who had spoken was pale and stocky, with a shaved head and mean eyes that made Ashe immediately dislike him. He nudged his friend with an elbow, mouth turning up into a smile that hinted at malice. "It's Frankie."

The other Diamondback was taller and slighter, with a warm complexion and black hair with a pronounced widow's peak. Unlike his companion, his expression was more guarded than malevolent as he stared at them.

"Hey, Frankie-girl," he said finally, his voice carefully neutral.

"Hi, Bez." Ashe didn't know Frankie well yet, but it was impossible to miss the hint of apprehension in her tone. "Zeke." The second name she said like it was a piece of bad food she wanted to spit out.

"Haven't seen you in months," Bez continued, taking a moment to size up Ashe as he spoke. "Thought you might have left town."

"Not yet," Frankie said simply.

"Aren't you going to introduce us to your new friend?" Zeke leered at Ashe.

"She can introduce herself." Ashe stood straighter and took a step forward. "Name's Calamity."

Bez's face softened briefly with surprise. "Calamity? The same Calamity who beat Dezba at Trout's the other night?"

"That's me." Ashe locked eyes with him. She wasn't sure what was going on here, but something felt off. Frankie used to run with the Diamondbacks, but not anymore. So did that make these two friends . . . or foes? Either way, she and Frankie didn't need the attention. Maybe a quick lie would get rid of them. "I'm building a new racing bike, and I've hired Frankie to help."

"So that's what you're doing now?" Zeke guffawed, an

obnoxious sound that made Ashe grit her teeth. "Wow, Marco is going to be livid when he finds out you're wasting time on that sort of—"

"Shut up, Zeke," interjected Bez. To Ashe's surprise, Zeke did just that, though he didn't look happy about it. Bez's mouth thinned a little, as if he was carefully considering what to say next. "He's right, though. Racing bikes? Really? Seems like a step down from being a Diamondback. Especially for someone with your talents."

"I guess some might see it like that." Frankie's voice was cool.

Once again, Bez regarded Ashe, as if she were a puzzle to be worked out. "Well, maybe when you're done with Calamity here, you'll give us another chance. Marco keeps asking when you're coming back."

Frankie's expression darkened. "Is he still running things the same as before?"

Bez nodded.

"Then never. I choose who I work with, and when. That was always the deal."

Ashe thought she saw the corner of Bez's mouth twitch up in the beginnings of a smile, but Zeke looked as if he just stepped in something awful.

"You should be begging him to let you come back," Zeke spat. "There's not another gang within five hundred miles of Bellerae that's better than—"

"These two bothering you, boss?" Jesse appeared suddenly, one hand resting on the butt of his revolver. Julian trailed warily behind him, a bulging satchel slung over his shoulder and some boxes at his feet.

Bez looked at Jesse, then back at Frankie and Ashe. "No need to start something, pretty boy. We were just saying hello to an old friend. Right, Frankie-girl?"

Some of the tension left Frankie's shoulders. "Yeah, right. Everything's fine, Jesse."

"She building you two a racing bike, too?" Bez didn't wait for them to reply, clearly smart enough to see beyond the half-truth. "We need to get going anyway. Marco hates when we're late getting back from a supply run."

"Then why don't you do that." Still somewhat confused by the interaction, Ashe was glad Jesse and Julian had shown up when they did. "Go on."

Again, Ashe caught a touch of amusement on Bez's face, but he obeyed.

"C'mon, Zeke," he said, leading the sour-looking Diamondback away. "Good to see you, Frankie. Really." There was a touch of genuine sincerity in the last word. "You ever want to get back to something other than making glorified toys, be sure to stop by."

As soon as the pair were gone, the air around them felt lighter.

"You okay, Frankie?" said Ashe. "What was that all about?"

Still looking a bit shaken, Frankie sighed. "Let's just say Marco, the leader of the Diamondbacks, wasn't exactly happy when I stopped working for them."

"Huh," said Julian, still watching the direction Bez and Zeke had gone. "I guess it's a good thing Marco wasn't with them then."

"You have no idea," said Frankie. "If we'd run into him instead . . ." She didn't finish the thought. "But you'll never find Marco doing any real work. He'd rather spend his time barking orders and feeling full of himself. That was Benito Sanchez—Bez—the gang's second-in-command. Marco may be the leader, but Bez is the one who makes sure they have things like food on the table and fuel in the gas tanks. He was also the only real friend I had when I was working with the gang."

That would explain Bez's careful interaction with Frankie, while Zeke had seemed bent on being inflammatory. "Still think he's your friend?" said Ashe.

Frankie looked unsure. "When I told him I was leaving, he didn't try to stop me. But he didn't understand, either. The Diamondbacks are the toughest gang around—to them that means everyone should want to be part of their crew. Unlike me, though, Bez doesn't have any other family or friends. And I just couldn't put up with Marco. So, I left."

Julian scoffed. "They didn't look *that* tough. I bet we could take them."

"We're not taking anyone," Ashe interjected. "We've got a plan to follow, and it doesn't involve the Diamondbacks. Did you get what we needed?"

Julian nodded and patted his satchel. "Right here and ready to go."

"Good. Then let's get the rest of the stuff and get out of here before anyone else runs into more 'old friends.'"

"Put it all over there," Ashe ordered.

B.O.B. obeyed, ferrying the items they'd acquired at Fort Starr to the back of the barn and depositing them in a neat pile beside the wrecked chopper from Cutthroat Trout's. Ashe eyed the assortment—it was everything they needed to pull her plan off. Now that they had the right parts, the challenge was going to be to get the bikes finished before the heist. It wasn't going to be easy, but if they got to work immediately, it would get done. Frankie and Julian were already hard at work, pulling what needed to be replaced off the four hoverbikes.

Ashe knew she should join them. And yet, the itch of another idea pulled at her. She plucked the old red gas tank from the pile. Frankie had given her a strange look when she'd asked Metal Mary to add it to their other purchases, but the hacker had been polite enough to not ask why Ashe had wanted it.

She wasn't entirely sure herself. But looking at it now, Ashe felt the same touch of vision as when she'd ordered B.O.B. to bring the crashed chopper home with them. She rubbed one thumb over the scratched-up angel wings painted on the tank's exterior as her gaze moved from the tank to the wreckage and back.

"You're not seriously thinking about fixing that old pile of scrap, are you?" Jesse came up beside her, helping B.O.B. with the last of their parcels. "That bike has got to be as old as our grandparents."

"Probably older," said Ashe. "The chassis model is from 1976. But old doesn't mean useless. Hell, that Viper rifle in the dining room shoots as straight as the day it was made. And this 'pile of scrap' has more character than those newer bikes ever will. It just needs a little work to bring that character out."

Jesse chuckled. "Ashe, what that bike needs is a decent burial."

She set the gas tank down. "Just because you can't fix it doesn't mean *I* can't."

"I didn't say I *couldn't* fix it. Only that I wouldn't bother."

"Afraid of a little hard work, McCree?" Ashe went over

to the chopper and sat so that she was perched on the edge of its seat. "Just you wait; I'm going to make this bike the envy of Bellerae. There won't be a racer, rival, or cop around who will be able to catch me when I'm on it."

Jesse rubbed his chin, still skeptical. Ashe expected him to keep teasing, but instead he said: "That sounds like a big job for one person."

"Nothing I can't handle." Ashe gave him an indifferent shrug. "Though I suppose it wouldn't hurt to have a hand."

Jesse grinned. "You asking?"

"You offering?"

He walked over to a worktable and picked up a wrench. "When do you want to get started?"

Right now. That's what Ashe wanted to say. Instead, she let out a sigh. There were more pressing concerns. "It'll have to wait a bit. That Arbalest shipment is coming in two days whether we're ready or not." There was repairing and rebuilding to be done, and if they *really* wanted to be prepared, she and Jesse needed to devote some time getting used to shooting from the back of a moving hoverbike. "B.O.B., put on some coffee. We've got a long night ahead of us."

CHAPTER 10

The sun beat down on the back of Ashe's neck as they waited, silently, on the crest of a ridge, watching the dark line of asphalt cutting through the desert below. Sweat beaded on the top of her lip; she wiped it away. Nearby, Julian squinted at the midday sun while Frankie leaned closer to her bike, and the miniature fan she'd wisely installed whirled along with the digital displays and holoscreen projectors.

What the hacker had done in such a short time was a marvel, really. The system she'd wired into her bike would allow her to break into just about any transport system, so long as Frankie was close enough. "Digital lassoing," she called it, as if her target were cows in a herd.

On the other side of Ashe, Jesse sighed loudly. "Next time can we find a lookout spot with some shade?"

"Thought you were used to the hot sun." Ashe peered through her field glasses as they scanned the horizon, looking for movement. "Seeing as I plucked you off a farm and all."

"Sure, but there I could usually take my shirt off to cool down."

Julian laughed. "Poor Jesse. Can't do that now. Wouldn't want to be a distraction."

Ashe kept her eyes on the road. "For who? The convoy's drones?"

"The lizards?" said Frankie.

"Maybe the vultures?" added Ashe. "Bet you'd look just *delicious* to them."

Jesse smirked, unfazed. "Hah, hah."

"All right, enough jokes." Ashe leaned forward on her bike. "Everyone ready?"

"Ready and raring to go," said Julian.

"Ready and bored to tears," said Frankie. "You've already asked that like five times. Is the convoy coming or not?"

"Any time now." Ashe's blood began to pulse with a mix of anticipation, excitement, and a little bit of fear. They all knew the plan. Once Frankie had a chance to hack the main transport vehicle, Ashe and Jesse would take point, engaging the convoy. The security drones would be a bigger challenge, since they had more firewalls and wouldn't be an efficient use of Frankie's skills. But Ashe and Jesse would make short work of them. Thanks to the extra stabilizers they'd added to the hoverbikes, shooting while riding had turned out to be more of a pleasure than a challenge.

That left their retreat, once they stole the drive with the schematics. Which is where Julian came in. It would be a bit of tricky timing, but the plan was to get away with their prize right as they reached the Brisco Tunnel. Then, once the convoy passed into it, Julian would blow the entrance with the explosive charges he'd set, covering their retreat.

It was a solid plan. Now all they had to do was execute it.

There was a faint flicker on the horizon, like the glint of sun on metal. Ashe zoomed in on it and inhaled sharply.

The convoy. Unmistakable, though still far enough out to be little more than a hazy blur.

She lifted the goggles onto her head. "Here they come! Julian, you get going to the tunnel. But stay on our channel." Frankie had outfitted them all with ear pieces they could use to communicate during the job. "And stay out of sight when you head down the ridge."

"On my way!" Julian gave her a cheeky salute before speeding off.

"Frankie?" said Ashe.

"They're almost in range," she said. "I'll let you know when I make a connection."

"Remember, don't stop anything." Stopping the vehicles would trigger an automatic alert to the nearby Arbalest factory, and they didn't want it sending help. "Once you do get into the system, stay close but not so close they bother with you. Jesse and I will take care of the rest."

Ashe's heart began to beat faster. Beside her, Jesse's face was alight with excitement. Trading a silent glance of mutual agreement, they revved their hoverbike engines and steered down the embankment, leaving Frankie to her work. With fresh gunmetal-gray paint jobs, the bikes looked almost new, though entirely nondescript. Gangs like the Diamondbacks and the Harpies might want to advertise their criminal accomplishments, but Ashe's schemes hinged on anonymity. For that reason, they'd also left B.O.B. behind. This payload didn't require his muscle, and it wasn't worth chancing the omnic being identified.

The terrain was rocky as they headed for the road. Fortunately, the hoverbikes had been designed with Cutthroat Trout's rough brand of racing in mind, so they'd come ready to handle whatever desert, steppe, or other ground their crew might encounter. But Frankie had added some bells and whistles, too—like a responsive autopilot setting, which kept the bikes following the line of the road and in proximity of their rider, in case any of them were separated from their vehicle. But if everything went smoothly, they wouldn't need that function.

Ashe adjusted the rifle slung over her shoulder as they approached the road. "Moment of truth, McCree. Try to keep up, okay?"

"Funny"—he winked at her—"I was about to say the same thing to you."

"Uh, Ashe—" Frankie's voice crackled a little with static. "Good news, bad news."

"Bad news?" Ashe stiffened. "What do you mean, bad news?"

"Good news first," Frankie said. "It's gonna be no problem 'lassoing' the controls on the main transport vehicle." She paused. "The bad news is that I don't know which one to hack."

Which one? Ashe sped up, steering to a raised spot of earth where she could see the road better. No need for the field glasses now; the convoy was close enough to pick out its individual parts. Immediately, she understood what Frankie was concerned about: Instead of one main transport vehicle, there were three, boxy black metal hulks traveling in a neat line, escorted by at least a dozen guard drones hovering at high speed alongside them.

Ashe swore.

"Abort?" said Frankie.

"Not a chance." Ashe pulled up her bandanna, and adjusted her hat to make sure her hair was still hidden. "The schematic drive is in one of those vehicles. And we're going to find it. Frankie, start with the one in the back. McCree, let's get moving!"

"You got it," said Jesse, falling in beside her.

Wind pulled at Ashe as she and Jesse began to fly over the landscape. They reached the asphalt and began tailing the convoy from about a hundred yards back. Then, moving in tandem, they switched over to autopilot before raising their rifles and firing. Two of the guard drones exploded.

That was it. There could be no mistaking their intentions now. The heist was on.

Immediately, the other guard drones tightened formation.

"No going back now!" cried Ashe.

She released her rifle and began to steer again, but Jesse fired once more, disabling another drone.

"Two for me," he called.

"It's not a contest, McCree."

He laughed low. "Sounds like something the loser would say."

A trio of guard drones disengaged from the convoy and headed straight for them, just as they'd expected would happen. Ahead, the road stretched out endlessly before them, the tunnel still out of sight, but Ashe knew it wasn't far. They'd have to work fast.

She swerved the bike as one of the drones fired at her, then flipped her rifle up again. One more shot, one less drone. Nearby, Jesse was also engaging again, but his shot glanced off his target as it fired on him and he was forced to duck. Ashe took aim and finished it off as the third and final drone surged at Jesse, getting too close for the rifle. Without missing a beat, he drew the revolver on his hip, firing once at point-blank range. A moment later, the remains of the drone hit the asphalt between their bikes, breaking into pieces they quickly left behind.

"Three to three," she called.

Jesse gestured with his revolver. "I thought we weren't counting?"

"Okay, I've got the rear vehicle," Frankie announced. "The top hatch is unlocked. All you need to do is get inside."

Sure, thought Ashe, accelerating on the convoy. *Nothing to it.* "Thanks, Frankie."

"Good luck," said the hacker.

"Don't need it, but I'll take it. Jesse?"

Jesse nodded, accelerating as well.

They approached the convoy, swerving as the remaining drones, split across the three transports, fired on them. But as close as Ashe and Jesse were to the back of the final vehicle, the drones didn't have a good angle. At least not without leaving their charges and exposing themselves.

"Cover me!" Ashe ordered, her mask hiding the wild grin on her face. This was even more exciting than racing. And though the stakes were higher, and the danger greater, she wasn't alone. Jesse, Julian, and Frankie—for the first time in her life, someone other than B.O.B. had her back.

A set of rungs ran up the back of the transport. She steered as close to it as possible, and set the bike to autopilot. Then she leaped. The sensation came with the briefest memory of jumping from the platform to the ladder during the first heist, but there was no fear this time. Only the thrilling feeling of achievement as she caught ahold of the transport and scrambled up it. As she reached the top, a guard drone suddenly appeared. There was no time for surprise, much less to react. Its weapon was barely feet away, pointed right at her.

Then it exploded, bits of hot metal showering her. Ashe yelped, clinging desperately to the ladder with one hand while swatting at her clothes with the other.

"Watch it!" she yelled at Jesse, who still had his rifle raised and ready.

"*You* be careful," he threw back. "I can't see the other one!"

A moment later, Ashe realized why. It had come down around the opposite side of the vehicle, appearing beside and below her, out of Jesse's view. There was no time to get in a position to use her own rifle. Instead, she held on tight and kicked out, striking the drone squarely with the heel of her boot. It plummeted and struck the road, bouncing along like a discarded tin can as the convoy continued on.

Ashe peeked over the top of the vehicle. The final few guard drones were staying where they were. Curious, but that was a puzzle she'd have to figure out later. The next part was going to be tricky. As soon as she broke cover, she'd be a target. But a glance back showed that Jesse was ready for that. He swerved to one side of the transport and began laying down cover fire. Immediately, Ashe climbed onto the roof and bolted to the hatch. Throwing it open, she took a fraction of a section to scan the inside for danger before jumping in. The interior was dim and confined, barely high enough for her to stand up straight, and fixed with armor plating on all sides.

It was also empty.

"Damn it!" Ashe scanned the space again, to be certain. "Nothing in this transport. Frankie, start working on the next one."

Tight with frustration, Ashe boosted herself back up onto the roof. The other drones still hadn't changed position. And worse, the tunnel was approaching. She could see it in the distance now, a gaping black maw at the base of a huge ridge of solid stone.

"We gotta move faster." Ashe turned to go back to the ladder. "Jesse, get ready to—watch out!"

It was the drone she'd kicked. Apparently, the fall hadn't been rattling enough to disable it, and now it was coming up behind McCree fast. Too fast. Ashe flipped her rifle up as Jesse turned to look behind him, knowing she couldn't move quickly enough and that the drone had Jesse dead to rights.

Then it exploded. Really exploded, the damage far worse than anything one of her bullets could have done.

"What the heck was that?" Jesse exclaimed.

"You all didn't really think I was just going to sit around while you have all the fun, did you?"

"Julian?" Ashe hollered. "You're supposed to be setting up the tunnel!"

"Already done!" Julian appeared, laughing as he swerved into her view. In one hand he held a stick of dynamite with some kind of detonator attached to it.

"See, Jesse? I told you these would come in handy." He reached back again and lobbed the stick toward the drones at the front of the convoy. It fell short, exploding as it hit the asphalt and leaving a smoking hole.

"You let him buy *dynamite*?" Ashe cried.

"Only a little," said Jesse.

"Not sure how I feel about that," Frankie said, over their comms.

"Me neither," said Ashe. "But I wanna see something. You got some more of those handy?"

Julian gave her a thumbs-up. "Sure do."

"Then wait for me and Jesse to get to the middle transport, and blow the last one."

Ashe descended the back of the transport, returning to her hovercycle, which had remained in close proximity. Taking opposite sides, she and Jesse advanced to the next vehicle in the convoy. As they passed the empty one, Ashe caught a glimpse of something arcing through the air toward the hatch she'd left open. Julian's throw was dead on. A moment later there was another explosion. Flames burst from the top of the vehicle, but it continued moving.

It was a gamble for sure. With one of the transports stopped, more Arbalest security would be on the scene within minutes. But Ashe's bet paid off: The remaining drones suddenly perked up again. The two guarding the middle transport suddenly abandoned it to surround the first.

"There!" Ashe shouted. The drones' formation told her all she needed to know. "Frankie, unlock the front vehicle, not the middle one."

"On it!" said Frankie.

"McCree?" Ashe glanced over at him and brought up her rifle.

"Let's finish it!" One hand on his own weapon, he accelerated.

Four drones left. They were almost to their prize—it was so close Ashe could feel the swell of victory rise within her.

Then a new drone suddenly appeared from atop of the first transport. Ashe's stomach plunged as another appeared behind it, and another.

"Uh, the first vehicle is open," Frankie said in a worried voice, "but I'm not the one who opened it."

"Yeah . . ." Jesse sounded as nervous as Ashe suddenly felt. "We see why."

A total of six more drones appeared. Beyond them, the Brisco Tunnel raced closer and closer.

"Ashe," Jesse continued, "we need to call it. We're not gonna make it in time."

No. They were so close. The new drones were a problem, but one they could solve . . . if they had the time. Which they didn't. "We're not giving up! Frankie, can you slow down the transports? Not stop them, just buy us another minute or two."

"You got it," Frankie replied warily. "But, Ashe, I'm still not sure that's enough—"

"It'll have to be," Ashe cut in. "Julian, how many more of those dynamite sticks have you got left?"

"Uh, four."

"Then this is what we're going to do," said Ashe. "Frankie, you slow them down a bit. Meanwhile, Julian, start throwing the dynamite at the drones. You don't need to disable them, just distract them."

"What are you thinking, Ashe?" said Jesse.

"The direct approach. I'm going for the lead transport." Ashe shouldered her rifle. "And I need you to cover me. Use the second transport as a shield."

He hesitated, but only for a moment. "You got it."

At that moment, the middle transport suddenly slowed, falling behind them. Ashe swerved into its place as Jesse slowed to match it, before accelerating on the final vehicle ahead, which had also reduced its speed. The guard drones responded by arranging themselves in two lines around it, the front shielding the back, but she got close enough to be out of their line of sight.

"Julian, Jesse, now!" Repeating what she'd done on the other transport, Ashe jumped from the bike to the ladder, and climbed.

As expected, a drone came for her when she did, but Jesse picked it off. An explosion sounded ahead, and close, followed by a second one. The distraction was enough to get her on the roof, but that was it. Lucky for her, McCree was keeping his eyes open. He picked off the two drones that broke formation as Ashe bolted forward, allowing her to get to the hatch and jump in.

This time, in the center of the transport sat a box, smaller than a suitcase. It wasn't even locked. Ashe threw it open and there it was: the schematic drive they were after.

Outside, the last of Julian's dynamite went off. "Hey, Ashe . . ." he said, sounding worried.

She closed the case and peeked back out of the transport. The tunnel was right ahead.

"Julian, get ready!" she cried, climbing back onto the roof, case in hand. "Frankie, speed the transport back up NOW."

"Now" came so fast that Ashe was nearly thrown from the roof of the transport. She stumbled, keeping hold of the case as she went down, rolling to the edge. And then she went over, hand grabbing a rung at the last moment. The drones were similarly thrown by the sudden change in speed, and abandoned their protective protocols in order to catch up. They flew by on either side of Ashe, apparently not realizing that what they were escorting was now in her grasp, and no longer inside the transport. But they would, any moment now.

The tunnel loomed.

"Jesse, disengage!" Barely taking a moment to steady herself with one foot on the ladder, Ashe jumped for her bike again. This time was far less graceful, but she managed it, grabbing for the handlebars and steering the bike off into the desert. The second transport passed her, and a moment later the tunnel swallowed both of the vehicles and what remained of their escort.

An explosion roared, shaking the ground around them so hard Ashe could feel it on the hoverbike. She ducked down as bits of stone and dust rained down around her, but she was smiling as she did so. Julian's timing had been perfect.

She stopped her hoverbike and took a long, deep breath.

"Ashe!" Jesse's voice yelled in her ear. "Ashe, you okay?"

"Couldn't be better." She laughed, turning to examine the pile of rocks and debris that now filled the entrance to the tunnel. Jesse was nearly to her, and she could see Julian and Frankie approaching on their bikes as well. She raised the case triumphantly so that they could see. "Now let's get out of here before those security drones figure a way out of that mess."

Internal Security Memo 126.7.54-B

ARBALEST

REPORT LEVEL—

NOT CLASSIFIED—YELLOW CLEARANCE

SUBJECT: BRISCO INCIDENT

Convoy carrying schematic files for upcoming H-29 scope engaged approximately seventy-five kilometers outside of Bellerae. Unknown number of assailants; minimum of two, though additional parties are suspected to have been involved. Firearms and munitions involved in hijacking. One transport and numerous drone escorts destroyed. Remains have been recovered and are currently being stored at Arbalest Fulfillment Center Beta-3.

Schematic files taken and no longer considered proprietary. Black market monitoring has yielded no further information leading to the identification of the thieves. Local biker gang activity suspected.

End.

BRISCO INCIDENT: EVIDENCE

PLAY ▶

STREAM Feed 32%

H-29 SCOPE

00:13:6524

CHAPTER 11

"And . . ." Frankie keyed a few more commands into the elaborate holoscreen system she'd set up in one corner of the barn. An old-fashioned cash register sound rang out. ". . . sold! Our first heist is officially a success."

A cheer went up throughout the barn. Or at least, as much a cheer as they could raise, given that there were only four of them. Five, if you counted B.O.B., who responded when Julian raised a hand to the omnic for a high five.

Ashe checked her tablet, refreshing the balance of the locked shadow account that Frankie had helped her set up. It was unhackable, untraceable, and accessible from anywhere in the world. She blinked for a moment at the new number, which filled the width of the screen. It wasn't as if she hadn't known how much they'd get for the schematics; after all, she was the one who'd set the price. But the hypothetical payment was very different from seeing the real one come through. It wasn't a fortune like the one she'd spent her whole life with access to, but it was a start. An excellent first step toward starting a new life.

"Way to go, everyone," said Ashe. "I know everything on the heist didn't go exactly as expected, but we rolled with the punches, and came out of it with everything we wanted. And, according to the Arbalest internal feeds, we're ghosts. They're attributing the theft to one of the local gangs, but they have no idea which one." With a few quick taps, Ashe made a series of transfers to several other accounts. "Most of this will stay in the main account, waiting to be split up once we're done. Some we'll put into equipment for the next job. But we all deserve a little fun money. It's only a taste, but there is more where this came from. A lot more." She turned the tablet around so they could see the amount.

Jesse gave a low whistle. "That's nothing to spit at."

"One job," Julian said, wide-eyed and speaking more quietly than Ashe had ever heard before. "That's from one job. I didn't earn half that in two years on the farms."

Ashe smirked. "And like I said, that's only the beginning. Arbalest isn't going to know what hit it."

Frankie practically glowed, the numbers on her screen glinting off her hologlasses. "I wanted to believe everything you said was possible, but this, this is . . . Ashe, do you understand how far we could go with the access you have? What we could accomplish with these resources? The sky is the limit!"

"Unfortunately, my *birthday* is the limit." Ashe felt a twinge of pain, and not the physical kind from the bruises she'd picked up on the job. "My parents will be back a week or two after that, and then I'm out on my own. But until then, we're going to take them for as much as we possibly– Geez, McCree, are you okay?"

Jesse was still staring at his account balance, a strange, slightly perturbed look on his face.

"Yeah," he said. "It's only . . . Well, I guess it's been a rough few years, and it's hard to believe this is real . . . almost like seeing the end of a long, dark tunnel."

Silence settled on them, and Ashe knew what they were all thinking about: the Omnic Crisis, and the devastating scars it had left–literally, in Julian's case.

"Yeah, it's been . . . rough," Julian agreed, with thoughtful hesitance.

Frankie looked down, her joyful expression gone.

They were right . . . they were all right. The war had been a dark time. And even though Ashe had been safer than the others, that safety had felt hollow, her loneliness deeper than at any other point in her life. Well, she wasn't alone now. And she had to say something. "I'm sorry." It sounded so trite coming from her. "I know I didn't experience the war like you all did, and I can't possibly understand. But still . . . I'm sorry."

"No, you can't." It was Frankie. "And consider yourself lucky because of that. My parents and grandparents. Two brothers. My auntie and her wife. We all lived in the same neighborhood, on the outskirts of Tulsa. Omnics hit it so hard it was like a wall of tornadoes went through. Our whole area was devastated. And we were some of the luckiest ones. We didn't lose anything that couldn't be replaced. We all walked away."

"I didn't," said Julian, fingers tracing the scarred patch along his cheek. "Walk away, I mean. But I was luckier than my parents. I got pulled from the rubble, spent over a month in a med camp recovering. After that, I was angry. I wanted in on the war." His eyes brightened a little. "And that's what happened. Gotta say, the education I got from the resistance group I hooked up with wasn't exactly conventional, but it's come in handy.

"What about you, Jesse?" said Frankie. "What's your story?"

Jesse kept his eyes downcast. "Not much to tell that you probably haven't heard before. So if you don't mind, I'd rather not tell it. The past is the past, y'know?"

The heavy silence returned, and Ashe felt an ache of guilt. Being disowned was trivial in comparison to what the others had gone through. What millions of people around the world had gone through. She could only imagine what might have happened if Overwatch hadn't come along and stopped the war. Jesse and Julian and Frankie? They already knew.

"But like I said"—Jesse looked up suddenly, his usual charmer's smile returning—"light at the end of the tunnel."

"Oh yeah?" Ashe met his gaze. "And what's beyond the tunnel?"

"Wherever I want, I suppose." He closed his eyes and leaned up against the wall of the barn, still smiling. "Reached by transcontinental rail, first class. A nice place to lay my head down and maybe a bit of land to work."

"A farm? Really?" She gave a short laugh.

One eye cracked open. "What's wrong with that?"

"Nothing," said Ashe. "Only I expected a bit more . . . ambition from you." She got up and went over to the hoverbikes, still dusty from the heist. Some of the drones' aim had been better than others, and both Jesse's and Ashe's bikes had picked up some fresh bullet holes in the fairings. "Julian, pass me a drill, would you? So, what are you going to do with all your ill-gotten but well-deserved gains?" she asked as he handed the tool over.

He struck an excited pose. "I'm gonna buy me a house like yours, to start. Okay, well, maybe not that big, but just as fancy. With handmade silk everything, a holoscreen television the size of this barn, and art made by dead folks whose names I can't pronounce. And when I'm bored, I'll blow stuff up in my huge backyard."

"Heck, we can do that now," Ashe said with a laugh. "Little explosions, though. Let's not get carried away." She started working on removing the damaged panels.

"Honestly, Ashe." Frankie turned off her holoscreen. "It won't kill you to take a break. We can do that in the morning."

"Won't kill me to get started on it, either." They were going to need better armor for the bikes before the next job. "What about you, Frankie? What are your plans?"

The hacker looked wistful for a moment. "First thing, I'm gonna send some of this money to my family. But later, I wanna help rebuild. Both where I grew up, and other places. There was so much destruction left by the Crisis, it's going to take decades to fix it all. The systems I could set up for community support and security . . . Let's just say I have plans." Then she smirked. "And I'm gonna travel, too. Anywhere I want. I'm gonna try food I've never tried, see things I've never seen, and hack networks that will never see me coming."

"Good plan," said Jesse. "But if we have to answer, so do you, Ashe. What are you going to do once this is over?"

Over. She hated the sound of it. The robbery was some of the most fun she'd ever had, and she was already looking forward to the next one, and what kind of challenges it would offer their crew. But she'd said it herself, soon enough her parents would be back, and she'd have to move on. The question was . . . where?

"I—I've never spent much time beyond Bellerae. I guess I don't really know what's out there for me." Was there anything? Like Frankie had said, there was a whole wide world to be explored. There must be someplace for her to go. No . . . there were a million places for her to go. The question was, where did she *want* to be? No answer sprung to mind, but that didn't matter. She didn't need to figure that out right now. "What I do know is that we've still got plenty of work to do."

Ashe was about to bring up the plans for the next heist on her tablet when she stopped, fingers hovering above the screen. Maybe Frankie was right. It wouldn't hurt to take a little break. "But that can wait until tomorrow. Let's head back to the house to get cleaned up. How does a night at Trout's sound?"

One long, hot bath later, Ashe couldn't stop thinking about Jesse's question. If only worry were as easy to wash away as dirt. But it lingered, stubbornly intruding on her attempt at relaxation and filling her with frustration as they made their way through the desert to Cutthroat Trout's. What did it matter where she went, so long as she had the funds to pay her way there? There was no need to have a plan; if she went to Paris and ended up hating it, there was always Shanghai. Or Singapore, or even Numbani, where omnics were welcome, and B.O.B. would be free of the shadow of the war.

So why did it feel like she needed to figure it out right now?

Ashe chewed over the thought as the truck bounced over the uneven terrain, but it was stubborn as a piece of gum, never getting any smaller no matter how much she worked it over. At least it was a beautiful night. They'd taken a pickup truck, and Ashe and Frankie sat in the bed along with B.O.B. while Jesse and Julian rode up front. Above them, the stars lay over the landscape like a blanket, twinkling faintly.

"No cards tonight," Jesse could be heard saying from the driver's seat. "You've got a terrible poker face."

"Not true," insisted Julian. "I've just had a run of bad luck lately. Anyway, I've been working on my strategies."

"No cards," Jesse said again. "And no aces up your sleeve, either."

"Julian might have saved Jesse earlier"—Frankie chuckled—"but it sounds like Jesse may have to return the favor before the night is out." When Ashe didn't respond, she continued. "Penny for your thoughts? Or do heiresses' cost more than that?"

"Just . . . thinking," Ashe responded.

"About what?"

Ashe hesitated. "About what to do. After . . . this."

"Aren't you the one who keeps telling us we'll be able to do whatever we want?" Frankie said. "Look, I know they say money can't buy happiness, but it can sure get you started in the right direction."

"Tell that to my parents. Their fortune certainly hasn't bought it yet. Though it has bailed me out more times than they'd like to admit." Ashe was silent for a moment. "Do you miss them?"

"Who?"

"Your family," said Ashe.

Frankie took a deep breath, and then let it out slowly. "Of course. Every day. But I can be of more use to them doing what I'm doing. My brothers are younger than me, so they're still with my parents, and the temporary housing they got after the war ended is barely big enough for the four of them."

"Do they know you're a hacker?"

A strange look came over her features—part amused, and part guilty. "They know enough. Which is probably more than I've told them, but less than would be incriminating."

Ashe chewed at the inside of her lip. "Do you think they'd disown you if they knew the truth?"

"Of course not! It's really more to protect—" Frankie said, before catching herself. "Shoot, sorry. I didn't mean it like that. Ashe, I don't know your parents or what it was like growing up with them, but . . . families are complicated. None of them are perfect."

"I know," said Ashe. "It's only that . . ." What? Why was she even asking Frankie about her family, anyway? "Never mind."

"Look," said the hacker gently. "During the war, and right after, there were a lot of people in my neighborhood who'd lost everything, including their families. But that didn't mean they were on their own—we all shared food, shelter, medical supplies . . . whatever we had. Sometimes family isn't about blood, it's about who sticks by you during the tough times. Just because your parents aren't sticking by you doesn't mean no one else ever will."

"I can manage on my own," Ashe said reflexively. Immediately, she regretted how curt it sounded. "But it's nice not to have to, sometimes."

"Yeah," said Frankie, with a knowing little smile. "It sure is."

Bellerae Daily Pioneer

PROUDLY SERVING THE COMMUNITY OF BELLERAE SINCE 1887   UPDATED 13:45

IS THERE A NEW GANG IN TOWN?

Following a string of brash, and successful, robberies in the Bellerae area, rumors are beginning to circulate about a new criminal enterprise setting their sights on local arms shipments. Several heists involving Arbalest shipments, as well as a handful of others from competitor companies passing through the region, have been confirmed. Sheriff Carson has been quiet on the subject, saying little more than there had been a minor uptick in recent criminal activity, but that it's not significant enough to draw any conclusions at this point.

Independent investigation has led to several local gang sources claiming responsibility for the heists. However, when pressed, none were able to provide enough details to confirm their involvement. Which leads the *Bellerae Daily Pioneer* to ask the question: Do we have a new gang in town? One that seems both elusive and well-outfitted for their plans? There are few details

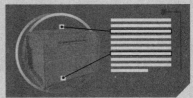

currently, including none that would help definitively identify the criminals, but local transports have been urged to take additional precautions for the time being.

BRAZEN DAYLIGHT HEIST CLAIMS SHIPMENT OF ARBALEST AMMUNITION

At least three suspects swooped down on an Arbalest truck shipment midday yesterday, making off with a dozen crates of high-end ammunition in a variety of calibers. The robbery took place in the foothills outside of Bellerae, about ten miles from Deadlock Gorge. According to witnesses, the transport was overcome by the sheer brazenness of the robbery, which was executed with clockwork precision.

No injuries were reported, though several guard drones were damaged or destroyed, and the truck driver was tied up for approximately an hour before assistance reached him. No descriptions of the masked robbers were provided other than the leader possibly sounded female, and that they made off with the ammunition on their hoverbikes.

When reached, an Arbalest spokesperson declined to comment, citing that they do not discuss open investigations involving their products or shipments.

Bellerae Da[ily] Pioneer

UPDATED 22:07

PROUDLY SERVING THE COMMUNITY OF BELLERAE SIN[CE

STORAGE FACILITY BROKEN INTO OVERNIGHT!

SURPLUS MILITARY-GRADE BODY ARMOR STOLEN

Sometime between midnight and 3 a.m. this morning, thieves broke into a local warehouse used by a number of Bellerae businesses and made off with several crates of surplus body armor. The surveillance cameras were disabled prior to the break-in, and no other evidence was found at the scene. Police questioned locals in the area about any unusual activity, but no one reported anything out of the ordinary.

CHAPTER 12

Business. Was. *Great.*

Ashe found it hard not to let the self-satisfaction fill her as she tightened a bolt on her chopper-in-progress. Over the last couple months, they'd executed nearly a dozen flawless (okay, nearly flawless) heists of Arbalest shipments. Thanks to Frankie's hacking skills, they'd even taken on a few other corporate shipments, so it wasn't entirely obvious that their focus was on Arbalest. But those had been peanuts, really, chosen because they were easy. Arbalest still made up the meat and potatoes of their operation, and their plates were growing more and more full with each job.

"The Vultures," said Jesse, perched on a pile of crates across the barn.

She shook her head. "No."

The crates were their latest score, an entire lot of the same Pantoptica field glasses she and Jesse had used during their first act of thievery. They'd snatched them a few days ago from a transport truck whose driver had foolishly left them unguarded while he ate breakfast at a greasy-spoon diner, one of their easiest heists yet. Ashe didn't love having them sit around the barn, but they had a buyer lined up. All they had to do was deliver them later this afternoon.

McCree stared into space, deep in thought. "The Copper Coyotes."

"Definitely not." Ashe held out a hand. "Screwdriver. Flathead this time."

Jesse got up and went over to the workbench, scattered with tools, and picked one out, handing it to her.

"Thanks." Ashe leaned closer to the bike, blowing dust away from the engine she was working on. Despite the mess it used to be, the chopper was shaping up nicely. Maybe, said a thought fluttering around Ashe's head, it was exactly the sort of vehicle she could ride out of Bellerae and never look back. "Why are you so dead set on a name for us, anyhow? It's not like we'll be using it for long."

Jesse made an exasperated noise. "Because 'mysterious, unknown gang' is so dull. Wouldn't you rather be known as something exciting, even if only for a while?"

"You sound as cheesy as the newspapers. What was it they wrote the other day? 'Watch out, Bellerae, there's a new gang in town. Precise, efficient, they swoop down like an owl at midnight, plucking their prizes and disappearing before anyone can stop them.'"

"That's it," said Jesse. "The Shadow Bats!"

Ashe couldn't help but laugh. "Wait, are we owls or bats?"

"Who cares? So long as we're something, led by the brilliant but mysterious Calamity."

Still clutching the screwdriver, Ashe shot Jesse an inquisitive look. "Brilliant but mysterious, huh?"

"Entirely true," he said. "And if Bellerae knew the true face *Calamity* kept hidden behind her mask, they'd be even more eager to put it on the Wanted posters. Too bad that would ruin the whole operation."

"Yeah," said Ashe. "Too bad." She still didn't quite think of herself as Calamity, but the identity had been a useful fiction. It helped that Frankie had done a fairly good job of scrubbing her picture from the *Daily Pioneer's* archives; any images from her arrest now appeared as broken links, or were outright deleted. "Though you never know—maybe they'd prefer to put the angelic face of Jesse McCree on those Wanted posters. 'He looked so young and innocent'"—Ashe affected a falsetto tone—"'who knows what drove him to a life of crime?'"

Jesse laughed. It was a sound Ashe had become accustomed to over the last couple months, deep and sincere. Frankie, on the other hand, had a chuckle that tended to turn into a snort, while Julian sometimes couldn't stop his laughter from sounding like a cackle. The halls of Lead Rose had sounded very different lately.

"Can't imagine my ugly mug ever making it onto a poster," he said finally, once he'd gotten his breath back.

Ashe returned to her work on the bike. "Oh, please—"

"Oh, please, *what*?"

Ashe tightened a screw. "You know very well what I mean."

"No, I don't." Jesse stood and moved a little closer to where she worked, smirking. "I really don't."

Ashe gave him a skeptical look and rolled her eyes. "Jesse McCree, are you trying to get me to say you're handsome when you *should* be finishing rebuilding that carburetor?"

The smirk widened. "Am I?"

Ashe shifted her features to wondering, and she thought for a long moment. Then she shrugged. "Don't know, you should probably ask Julian or Frankie."

He wilted just a little, but it was extremely satisfying to see.

"Or B.O.B.," Ashe continued. "Hey, B.O.B., do you think Jesse is handsome?"

The omnic put out a hand, palm down, and rocked it back and forth—the universal gesture of "meh."

"Well, whatever you look like now, it's gonna get a lot worse if you don't finish preparing those crates for the hand off."

"They're not ready yet?" Julian, with Frankie behind him, appeared in the barn doorway. "C'mon, it's almost time to go, McCree."

"Yeah," said Frankie. "And time, as they like to say, is money."

Jesse opened his mouth to say something—undoubtedly snarky—but Ashe cut him off.

"You heard 'em, McCree." All fun aside, it was time to get down to business. "Get moving!"

The rendezvous spot was about an hour outside of Bellerae, at an outcropping of rock locally known as "The Hopper" since it resembled a crouching rabbit with its ears pressed back. The sun was getting low and the shadows stretched out, drawing dark lines across the landscape. They'd arrived early, and the others—including B.O.B.—lounged around on the pile of crates as Ashe kept watch. It hadn't been easy, figuring out a way to bring the omnic without the help of a truck, but finally Frankie and Ashe had modified a pair of hover-transport platforms that could be hitched to the back of their bikes. One for cargo, one for B.O.B. Problem solved.

Suddenly, Ashe spotted a large van making its way over the road. Unlike the handful of other vehicles she'd seen, this one turned into the desert, heading right toward them.

"Frankie, that your guy?" Ashe handed the hacker her field glasses, but Frankie waved them away.

The tint on her hologlasses shifted slightly. "Yup, I'd know that truck anywhere. Right on time."

Like Metal Mary, the buyer was someone Frankie had worked with before; he'd offered a fair price on the whole lot with the plan of selling them (at a respectable profit, of course) through his East and West Coast city contacts. A nice, clean transaction to complete their latest heist.

The truck rolled to a stop about ten meters away, the setting sun behind it. A tall, skinny man wearing a spotless white jacket and leather pants exited. Despite the fading light, he had on a pair of dark sunglasses, and flashed them a toothy grin as he approached.

"Frankie, baby." He pulled off the shades and held his arms out in a wide, welcoming gesture. "Great to see you again."

"Hey, Liu," said Frankie. "Thanks for meeting us out here."

"Not a problem," Liu said. "What's a little drive when there's good business to be had?" He turned to Ashe. She had her Calamity persona on—red wig, with a bandanna pulled up over her face—same as all the others, save Frankie. He lingered on her for a moment before moving on to Jesse and Julian, then back to Frankie. "I see you've made some new friends. I'd ask your names, but are those really important?" He snickered at his own joke. "Those the goods there? May I inspect them?"

"Of course." Ashe went over and opened one of the crates.

Inside were rows of field glasses, nestled neatly in a bed of protective foam.

"Oh yes," said Liu, drawing out the s sound. "That's the kind of quality I like to see. Now, how about getting a hand loading these crates?"

Ashe snapped her fingers at B.O.B., who lumbered over and picked up a crate. "Not a problem. We're happy to provide a full-service experience for our customers."

"Fine goods and prompt service." Liu sounded pleased. "This is a very different operation from your last one, Frankie."

"Day and night," said the hacker as B.O.B. continued to load the crates into the truck.

When that was done, Liu raised the wrist device he wore. "Complete transfer," he spoke the command into it, "Authorization code: purple polka-dotted glitter toads."

Frankie's hologlasses flickered briefly. She nodded the confirmation at Ashe. "It's all there."

Ashe smiled beneath her bandanna. "Nice doing business with you, Mr. Liu. Maybe we can work together again sometime."

But instead of looking pleased, Liu's confident demeanor suddenly shifted. He looked around furtively, fussing with the sunglasses in his hands. "If only that was possible." He turned back to Frankie. "Sorry, Frankie, baby. Look, the money is good, but, I— well, they gave me no choice."

Ashe went cold. "Frankie, what is he talking about?"

"Who gave you no choice?" Frankie demanded, shocked. "Liu, what did you—"

It was then that they heard the engines—lots of them. The sound came from all around, echoing off the stone formations surrounding them.

Jesse's face turned more serious than Ashe had ever seen. "We need to go."

"We need to go *now*," Julian punctuated, starting for his hoverbike.

But it was already too late. A dozen riders on bikes appeared and surrounded them like a pack of metal wolves, blocking every avenue for escape. Despite the dusk, enough light shined from their headlights to illuminate their insignia as clear as day: Diamondbacks. As they came to a stop, Ashe could see that they were well armed, most carrying rifles or revolvers, as well as knives on their belts.

Frankie swore. "Ashe, we have a problem."

"No kidding," said Ashe, through her teeth.

Whatever this was, it couldn't be good. The tense encounter at Fort Starr hadn't bothered Ashe at the time; after all, they'd had no reason to cross paths with the gang again, or to be involved with them in any way.

So what was this?

There was one bike that was more decorated than all the others, with the gang logo emblazoned on the front, along with what looked like a splash of red paint.

At least, Ashe hoped it was paint.

The rider of that bike dismounted, swaggering over to where Ashe and the others were corralled in the center of the Diamondbacks' circle. As he walked, he removed his helmet, revealing a youngish man, maybe six or seven years older than Ashe. He had dark brown hair trimmed in a severe, almost military style and sharp features. Another Diamondback followed him, keeping a few deferential paces behind: Bez.

"Frankie!" the young man said, sounding faintly amused. "Long time no see."

Frankie looked like she'd bitten into an apple only to find a worm inside. "Marco. What are you doing here?"

Marco looked playfully pained. "What kind of greeting is that? Especially after we came all this way. I see that you've found some new friends, but have you forgotten your old ones so quickly? Speaking of which"—he turned to Liu—"take off. You're done here."

The dealer wasted no time. He fled from the gathering, climbed into his truck, and sped off, disappearing into the falling night.

Ashe's jaw tightened further as the lights of Liu's vehicle faded. No one else knew they were meeting with Liu; he'd betrayed them. The feeling of it scorched her insides. And Marco was already grating on her nerves. He had a mean look to him, but the kind of mean that told her he probably bullied others to get what he wanted. She didn't like bullies, especially ones who got in the way of her plans.

"Can we help you . . . " Ashe crossed her arms, glaring. "What was it? Marco? As I'm sure you can see, we're trying to conduct business here."

"Don't," hissed Frankie.

On the other side of her, Jesse gave her a nudge and a none-too-subtle shake of his head. Ashe ignored both of them as Marco took a step forward, looking her over. He got uncomfortably close, so near that she could have reached out and touched him.

"I see that." The Diamondback's leader sounded less

than thrilled. "Which would be why I'm here. You're the one called Calamity, right?"

Ashe nodded, holding his gaze.

Marco sniffed derisively, seemingly unimpressed. "My buddy Bez here says you raced down at Cutthroat Trout's, and that Frankie is helping you build a bike. Isn't that right, Bez?"

"Yeah, that's what she *said*." There was a hit of bitterness in Bez's voice.

"Which," Marco continued, "sounded a bit suspect, given what Frankie is usually involved with." His nasty grin widened. "So I asked around a little and—lo and behold—here we are. Conducting business that is most definitely not of the bike-building sort."

Ashe flushed, her cheeks prickling with anger and warning.

"So," Marco said, "the four of you are the mysterious gang who has been working so hard around Bellerae lately. And from the way you talk, it sounds to me like you're the one in charge, Calamity."

"Uh," Julian injected, "she's the boss, sure, but when it comes to splitting the take, it's really more of a democra—"

"Shut up!" snapped Marco.

Julian's mouth promptly closed.

"Now," said Marco. "We need to have a little chat about what you've been up to."

His features hardened as he leaned closer to Ashe. Before she could pull back, he reached for her bandanna and yanked it down.

"You two," Marco barked at Jesse and Julian. "Masks off."

They hesitated, but Ashe gestured for them to obey. They pulled the fabric down.

Marco gave them a cutting smile. "Ah, there we are. Young lot, all of you. I remember how ambitious I could get when I was younger, too." He straightened and crossed his arms. "Now, I'm going to be nice about this, because I like Frankie, and I want to show what a good guy I can be. You four have been working hard, but that's done now. This is our territory—*my* territory—and you've gotten too greedy. Game over. This is the last payday you score, the last shipment you move."

The hell it was. Ashe started to speak, but something in his face stopped her.

"Whatever you're about to say, Frankie can tell you it's a very bad idea," Marco said. "Isn't that right, Frankie?"

The hacker chewed her lip nervously. ". . . Right."

Marco looked pleased. "I knew I could count on your honesty. Especially after I so kindly let you walk away from the Diamondbacks without any trouble. You don't want any trouble, either, do you, Calamity?"

"No, I don't." Ashe kept her voice cool, even a little cordial.

"But let me get this straight, are you asking us to give up on our heists because you think you have some claim to them, or because we're simply better at thieving than you are?"

Marco's mouth dropped open, then shut immediately, his features crumpling with annoyance. Ashe suppressed the urge to smirk at him. She remained quiet, waiting for his response.

"I know I said I was going to be nice "—Marco got right in her face, so close that Ashe could smell the sour hint of his breath—"but you are testing my patience. You do not want to cross me, Calamity. There's a lot of desert out here, a lot of places to dig holes. And people disappear every day. Would anyone even notice if the lot of you went missing?" His words, or their tone, caused B.O.B. to take a warning step forward, but Ashe held up a hand, signaling the omnic to keep back. "Now . . . do we have an understanding, *Calamity*?"

No, they did not, and Ashe wanted nothing more than to turn B.O.B. on him. It would be oh so satisfying to see a metal fist knock the superior look off Marco's face. But even with the omnic, and the fact that she and McCree were probably worth three of the Diamondbacks each, they were still dangerously outnumbered.

"Hold on," said Julian, coming forward, hands held up where Marco could see them. "There's no need for threats.

Marco, you look like a man who likes a good deal. And this crew? Well, this crew knows how to get its hands on some really choice—"

Marco struck like a snake, driving his fist into Julian's face. Julian cried out and fell to his knees, clutching his nose as dark blood leaked through his fingers. Jesse rushed to his side, only to jump up again and glare at Marco with a viciousness in his eyes that Ashe didn't like. Not one bit.

She stepped between him and Marco. "Jesse, no."

"What?" Jesse growled. "You're just going to let him get away with that?"

"I said *no*, McCree," Ashe repeated, putting more steel in her words this time.

Reluctantly, Jesse backed down.

"Frankie," Marco said, rubbing his knuckles, "come here."

"Don't listen to him, Frankie," said Ashe.

But the hacker, looking vaguely ill, went over to Marco.

"Now I'll ask you one more time . . ." Marco grabbed Frankie suddenly, twisting her around so that she faced Ashe and the others. A knife appeared in his free hand. "Do we have an understanding?" Frankie let out a small cry of surprise as he ran the tip of the blade lightly down her arm, then went dead still, eyes wide with fear.

For a moment, they all went silent, no one daring to speak.

Then Bez put a hand on the gang leader's shoulder. "Hey,

Marco. We like Frankie, remember? Just a warning, you said. There's no need to—"

Marco shrugged him off, keeping his gaze on Ashe. "This *is* a warning. So, what do you say, Calamity?"

Ashe swore to herself. Every inch of her screamed to fight, and from the look on McCree's face, he wanted to do the same. But this wasn't a battle they could win.

"Sure, Marco." Ashe kept her voice carefully even. "We have an understanding."

"Good." Marco released Frankie and shoved her back toward the others.

Ashe caught her. "Are you okay?"

Frankie nodded, shaken. "Yes . . . yes, I'm fine."

Marco laughed. "And so long as your little gang behaves, she'll stay that way." He returned to his hoverbike and revved the engine. "Remember our understanding, Calamity. Or next time I visit you, it's not gonna end as nicely."

A few yards away, Bez hesitated, an uncertain look on his face as the other Diamondbacks began to rev their engine, too. For a moment, it looked as if he might say something. Then he spun on one heel, going back to his own bike. Marco steered back toward the road, the other Diamondback riders following, one by one, Bez taking up the rear. Ashe watched until they were well away, and the only thing she could hear was Julian's whimpers of pain.

"What an ass," she said loudly. "Julian, you gonna make it?"

"He broke my nose." Julian wiped at the blood. "For no reason!"

"Like that's never happened to you before," said Jesse, but not without sympathy. "It ain't broken. I know a broken nose, and that's not it. We'll get you patched up at Lead Rose."

"We sure will." Ashe crouched beside him. "And then we're going to get back to planning the next heist."

"What?" Frankie blinked at her. "After what Marco said? After what he *did*?"

"Sure," said Ashe. "I heard all of that hot air. But I don't see why we should stop just because he's jealous that we're doing better than he could ever hope to."

"Ashe, this is serious." Frankie lowered her voice, nearly pleading. "Marco doesn't play around. Why do you think I didn't want to keep working with the Diamondbacks? Marco is dangerous. There's no telling what he'll do."

Ashe narrowed her eyes. She could still see the lights of the hoverbikes in the distance, moving away from them. "I don't like bullies. Marco is a bully. And not a smart one. The only reason he found us tonight is because Liu betrayed us. We won't make that mistake again. No more old acquaintances, no more searching for buyers at Trout's, and we check and double-check the credentials before we sell anything to anyone."

Frankie made an exasperated noise. "Seriously, Ashe, this isn't a joke. We're lucky we aren't digging our own graves right now. Marco's done worse over less."

"I know," she said. "Really, I understand. But we're nearly done, aren't we? Time is almost up, but we can still squeeze in a few more jobs, and I'm not gonna let that blowhard get in our way." Still, Frankie looked perturbed. "We'll be more careful. Besides, I've got my eye on something *big*."

Jesse and Julian looked up at her, expectant, and even Frankie's features softened, changing from fear to a conflicted sort of interest.

Never underestimate the promise of a hefty payday, Ashe thought.

"Oh yeah?" Jesse helped Julian get back up onto his feet. "What's that, Ashe?"

She smiled. "The heist we've been waiting for. The one that's gonna make all this well worth it, and then some." She paused a moment to let the words sink in. "Y'all, it's time for the big score."

REWARD

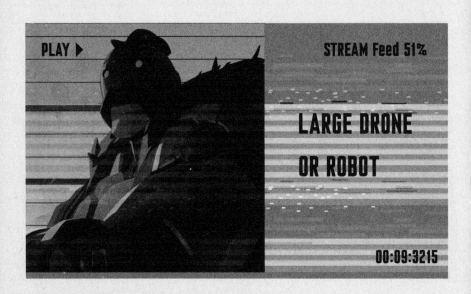

PLAY ▶   STREAM Feed 51%

LARGE DRONE

OR ROBOT

00:09:3215

$10,000

Offered for information leading to the identification and apprehension of unknown hovercycle gang currently targeting area shipments of weapons and ammunition in the Bellerae area. No identifying details are currently available, though gang may employ a large drone or robot for moving stolen cargo. Anyone with information should contact Sherriff Carson at the Bellerae Police Department.

Internal Security Memo 405.X.TS-X

ARBALEST

REPORT LEVEL

CLASSIFIED—BLACK CLEARANCE

SUBJECT: BELLERAE INCIDENTS

Recent string of Arbalest shipments no longer considered unrelated. Local gang activity confirmed, with strong suspicion of specific targeting of Arbalest shipments. Increased security measures have proved ineffective, possibly even adjusted for. No further security changes to be initiated at this time. Traditional information sources no longer considered useful in identification of assailants; however, alternative possibilities have been presented and are currently being explored. All further internal communications on this subject to be suspended for the time being.

End.

CHAPTER 13

It was a cool, clear night, with a bright full moon casting a milky glow over everything. Sure, it made them easier to see as Ashe and the others kept low, moving through the scrub toward the transcontinental railway stop, but that wasn't a problem in this case. The railway station, a starkly out-of-place geometric structure of high white walls and a dome made of webbed metal, was still under construction, currently used only as a way station for cargo and out-of-service railcars. Of the handful of trains currently using this line, most passed it without stopping, on their way to more interesting places. Save for a handful of security drones buzzing quietly by every so often, it was deserted. Not the sort of place where anyone would store a valuable weapons shipment.

Which was part of the brilliance of it.

And to think, Ashe had almost missed it. If she had, they would have missed out on the most fantastic opportunity yet. This was it—the heist that was going to fill their bank accounts all the way to the brim. But along with the financial gains, it came with an added bonus: a way for Ashe to take her revenge on her parents to a new level. Because if there was one thing her parents couldn't stand, it was being embarrassed.

Ashe knew that better than anyone.

So when she'd spotted something odd in an upcoming Arbalest shipping manifest, she'd followed up on it, picking through serial numbers and inventories until she figured out what she was looking at. And it was the information she found that set her heart pounding with excitement.

While it was true that her parents mostly stayed out of the day-to-day projects at Arbalest, there were always a few pet projects they kept their eyes on. Specifically, anything they could try and market to the megacorporations they spent so much of their time sucking up to. And as it turned out, Arbalest had a new cutting-edge energy cannon design it was ready to start showing off. Code name: Siren.

There were only a handful of specs and a basic schematic in the files, but what Ashe read left her nearly salivating. A weapon like this was worth a fortune on the black market, even if it was only a prototype.

According to the documents Ashe had found, the energy cannon was going to be secretly shipped to New York City, from the very warehouse that she and Jesse had first robbed. A demonstration was slated for next week in New York, and though there weren't any details about who the demo would be for, Ashe knew there was no way a meeting of that level was going to take place without her parents in attendance.

It would have been a great target just knowing the prototype's value. But the thought of the shipment never arriving, and the embarrassment her parents would experience when their customers found them empty-handed? That was the perfect cherry on top.

All they had to do was steal it.

She pulled up her bandanna and hefted a bag of supplies onto her shoulder. "Y'all ready?"

Julian nodded. "You betcha."

"When am I not?" said Frankie.

McCree adjusted his own mask. "Let's get moving, then. That shipment isn't going to steal itself."

"Now there's an idea," said Julian. "We should reprogram some drones to do the hard work for us."

"Where's the fun in that?" Leading the way, Ashe crept out from behind the rocky outcropping.

It wasn't going to be easy getting in. The train platform, with its glassed-in waiting area leading to whatever amenities were inside the main station, they ignored. And the gate to the cargo storage area, which was where they really needed to be, was solid metal, with numerous locks and sensors that would send an alert if they tried to open it.

Which they had no plans of doing.

No, this job was going to be less breaking and entering than scaling and infiltrating. At least at first.

But that first part would be hard enough. Ashe stared up at the walls of the rail station, a dizzying twenty meters above. From the base, she could just see the edge of the metal dome, designed in a pattern that Ashe was sure the rich train travelers passing by found aesthetically pleasing. She, on the other hand, was less than enamored by it, mostly since it was electrified to the point that it would turn any of them—maybe even B.O.B.—into a crispy critter with a single touch.

"Okay, here we go." Frankie kept her voice low as she crouched on the ground, leaning over a tablet. "The security drones won't be back around for another half an hour. So that's our time frame."

Jesse eyed the wall with reservation. "Might be tight."

"We'll make it." Ashe dropped the bag beside her.

Julian and Jesse did the same with the ones they carried,

pulling out lengths of climbing rope and the grappling guns they'd use to launch them.

Frankie swore in a low hiss.

"What?" said Ashe.

"It's the electrified webbing. I figured I could cut it to this sector no problem, but there's a fail-safe that reconfigures the power source if any part goes dead for more than a few minutes at a time. I can keep ahead of the system if I stay at it, but . . ." She looked up, the moon reflecting off her hologlasses. "Be careful. I won't be able to monitor the drone movement while you climb with this occupying me. But should be clear sailing once you get over the wall."

"No problem"—Ashe readied her grappling gun—"B.O.B., keep watch for her."

The omnic nodded.

"Just watch where you're sitting when it's time for us to go," said Julian.

As Frankie turned back to the tablet, Ashe, Jesse, and Julian took aim.

"Don't shoot too high," Ashe warned. Then she fired.

Julian and Jesse followed suit, their ropes rising into the air. A moment later, the pitons on the other end of them sank into the wall, near its top edge.

Ashe gave her rope a tug to test it. It held tight. "Frankie?"

"Electricity is cut. You're good to go."

"Okay, boys, let's get climbing." Ashe didn't bother to wait as Jesse and Julian secured the straps of their bags across their chests.

It wasn't easy going, and before she was halfway, Ashe's arms began to burn. She paused to rest, glancing around to get her bearings. The ground suddenly seemed much farther away than it had been a moment ago. Her grip tightened on the rope.

"What's the matter, Ashe?" Jesse came up beside her. "Too high for you?"

"Not a chance," she threw back. "Just taking in the view."

Jesse grinned and nodded at the top of the wall. "It'll be even better up there."

"And way nicer than looking at Jesse's backside," added Julian.

Ashe laughed, but there was no time for teasing. "C'mon. Last one to the top has to change the oil on all the bikes."

That got them moving. Soon, they reached the top, where there was just enough room between the edge of the wall and the metal webwork for them to stand. Barely.

Jesse eyed the structure skeptically. "We're sure this section is turned off, right?"

Julian pulled a pair of cutters out of the bag he carried. "I sure hope so. One set of burn scars is enough for me."

"It's off," Frankie insisted, through their earpieces.

"Here. I'll do it, you cowards." Ashe snatched the cutters away from Julian.

She wouldn't deny hesitating slightly as she closed the blades on a slim rib of metal, but it cut quickly and neatly, without cooking her to a crisp. Moving rapidly, Ashe cut a hole large enough for them to get to the other side.

"Be careful," said Ashe, passing through it.

"You *sure* you're not afraid of heights?" teased Jesse as he followed. "This isn't even that—" He faltered as his shirt snagged a bit of the metal, stumbling forward as he tried to regain his balance. Only, there was no place for him to go.

Except down.

Ashe grabbed for him, fingers barely snagging his collar in time. She yanked him back from the edge.

For a moment, there was only silence, though Ashe would have sworn she could hear the thump of Jesse's heart. And hers, too.

"I'm not afraid of heights." Ashe's momentary panic dissolved into relief. "Falling, on the other hand . . ."

Jesse flashed her his charmer's smile. "Thanks. That would have been a bad way to end the job, huh?"

Ashe shrugged. "Eh, we would have gone on without you."

They pulled up their lines and ran them down the inside

of the wall before descending. Solid earth under her feet again, Ashe relaxed a little.

"Okay," she said quietly. "Jesse and I will find the rifles. Julian, you work on our exit."

"Got it," said Julian.

She and Jesse plunged into the maze of crates and cargo containers. They took turn after turn, knowing what they were looking for was close, but there was a lot to search through. And it didn't help that the nest of shadows cast by the cargo made the whole place a little creepy. For a moment, Ashe couldn't shake the thought that they were walking through a graveyard filled with giant tombstones. But it was only metal and polymer, she told herself, and they sure as heck weren't grave robbers.

"Hey, over here!" Jesse hissed, keeping his voice low as possible.

Ashe rushed over, adrenaline racing as she spotted the familiar-looking Arbalest transport crate. It was one of the smallest items in the yard, and yet she knew it had to be one of the most valuable.

"That's it." She ran her fingers over the logo embossed in the top, right above the shipment number that confirmed it was what they were looking for.

"Now all we have to do is get it out of here," said Jesse.

"After that climb, it should be a—"

A sharp blaring noise cut through the night. In an instant, a dozen spotlights lit up, flooding the area with bright white light. Night disappeared; suddenly, it was almost as bright as daytime.

Jesse stiffened. "Spoke too soon."

"Frankie?" Ashe barked. "Julian? What's going on?"

"Sorry!" Julian came tearing around the piles of crates, gasping for breath. "Sorry, sorry, sorry!"

"What happened?" cried Ashe.

"I was setting up . . . the exit . . ." Julian panted. "Got too close to a service door . . . Think there was a movement sensor—"

"Did you set the charges?"

He nodded furiously.

"Then we're not caught yet." Ashe felt the adrenaline rise in her once more, but for worse reasons this time. "Grab the other end of this crate, McCree, and let's go!"

She grabbed one handle as Jesse grabbed the other, and they headed back out of the maze as quickly as they could, following Julian's lead.

"What's going on?" Frankie voice crackled in their ears.

"We got the goods and we're coming," said Ashe. "Move away from the wall!"

They made it to where they'd come in, their ropes still dangling. Farther down the wall, Julian had set up a ring of charges.

"Wait." He stopped them before they got too close. "Get behind that stack of crates!"

The three of them crouched behind it, covering their ears as Julian raised the detonator and pressed it. The klaxons disappeared beneath the explosion, and bits of concrete and dust began to rain down. But there was no time to wait for it to clear. In a flash, they were up again, running to the freshly made hole in the wall.

They stopped.

"Oh no," said Julian.

The bombs had taken out a huge chunk of the barrier, but they hadn't gone all the way through.

"I thought you said you brought enough explosives?" Ashe yelled at Julian, who looked bewildered.

"I thought I did!"

"Now what?" said Jesse.

There was no time to be mad. Or even to think.

"C'mon," ordered Ashe, pulling the crate, and by extension, Jesse, back toward the ropes. "Julian, you have an extra rope in your bag, right?"

"Yes," he said. "But–"

"Be quiet and listen to me," Ashe ordered. The alarms

were still going off, and that explosion was going to bring the security drones any second. "We'll tie one of the ropes to the crate. You use another to climb the wall. When you get to the top, tie the one with the crate to the extra rope, then throw it down to B.O.B. He can pull it up."

Julian looked unsure, but he ran for the nearest rope and began scaling the wall. He wasted no time reaching the top. While he worked, Ashe looped the end of another rope through one of the crate's handles and tied it off.

"Ready!" Julian called down.

"Here, too," Ashe replied. "B.O.B.! Pull!"

The rope went taut, and a moment later the crate began to slide up the wall.

"Okay," said Ashe, taking the rope Julian had used and holding it out to Jesse, "it's our t–"

"Ashe, get down!"

Jesse tackled her and they fell to the ground as gunfire peppered the area. A split second later, Jesse pushed away from her, rolling onto his back and drawing his revolver, firing rapidly at the security drone that had appeared above them. It was different from anything they'd encountered before, a sinister sort of flattened sphere with a glowing red line of optics and a pair of spidery appendages. Its matte gray exterior sparked as Jesse's bullets pierced it and it plummeted to the ground.

Jesse let out a breath, then looked up at the bullet holes peppering the wall where they'd been standing only moments ago. He actually looked rattled.

"C'mon. There will be more any second."

They jumped to their feet and began to climb again. When they reached the top, Ashe risked a glance over her shoulder. More security drones were headed their way, sweeping through the crates in a search for intruders.

"Faster, Ashe!" Jesse called.

"I hear you!"

They slipped through the hole in the webbing. The crate had reached the top as well, and together they navigated it through the hole. There was no time to be careful, though.

"I hope this thing has good padding inside," said Jesse as they unceremoniously dropped it over the other side.

Below, B.O.B. stood ready, plucking it from the air as it fell.

"Nice catch!" Ashe called down.

They began their descent, slipping down the rope far faster than Ashe liked. But a welcome sight met her below: Frankie had remotely called the bikes. The vehicles came racing toward them, pulling alongside the wall right as Ashe reached the ground. Quick as lighting, Frankie and Julian lashed the crate to the transport platform hitched behind Frankie's bike as B.O.B. climbed onto the one behind Ashe's.

"Julian!" Ashe and Jesse grabbed their rifles. "I'm gonna need to shoot, so you take B.O.B. and my bike. I'll take yours."

As they sped away from the rail stop, Ashe switched the bike to autopilot. It would follow Frankie's like a duckling after its mother. Nearby, Jesse did the same, and they spun in their seats, raising their rifles in unison.

And right in time. Four of the red-eyed security drones exited from a hatch in the wall and headed straight for them. Ashe fired, making short work of one, though her next shot went wide. Jesse took down another one with three shots in rapid succession. Then they both fired at once.

The last two drones exploded, their remains careening into the dirt.

There were more, no doubt, but they were already well away from the rail stop, with the night closing in around them. Still, it was another half hour before they all pulled to a stop in the curve of a steep ridge.

With no lights or sirens trailing, Ashe let herself breathe a sigh of relief. The heist had turned into a bit of a mess, but it was nothing they couldn't handle these days. Her eyes fell on the crate. And they'd made it out with their prize.

"Hope this thing is worth it." Julian swung off Ashe's bike, still looking a bit shaken.

"You bet it is." Ashe licked her lips greedily. "Frankie, give the crate a scan first for explosives."

"Although if there are any," said Jesse, "at least we might stand the chance of running away this time."

"It's clear." Frankie tapped the screen of her tablet. "And now it's unlocked. Ashe, you want to do the honors?"

"You bet I do." Ashe leaned over the crate and swung the lid open.

At first, she couldn't tell what she was looking at. Then logic kicked in, years of Arbalest knowledge embedded in her brain identifying the sight even as her mouth dropped open in surprise. This was no cutting-edge energy cannon prototype. The crate was filled with rifles, the standard-issue kind from the crisis, barely worth the materials they were made of.

"Those . . ." Disappointment flattened McCree's tone. "Those don't look like they're going to sell for much."

Julian snorted. "Those aren't even worth the scrap they're made of. Where's the supersecret new weapon?"

"I—I don't understand." Ashe's mouth closed and opened again. "It's the right crate. But this isn't what was on the shipping manifest."

"Hold on," said Frankie. "There's a local version of the manifest downloaded into the crate's memory. Let me see what it says."

She scrolled a bit, and then read off the number of the

crate, the one Ashe had seen on the shipping manifest back at the mansion. But what it contained definitely didn't match up.

Ashe felt like a balloon stuck with a pin.

"It must've been a mistake," said Frankie, in a soft, conciliatory manner. "A typo or error in the files."

Ashe shook her head. "But I–I checked . . ."

"It makes sense, Ashe." Jesse laid a hand on her shoulder. "It was a little too good to be true, a valuable shipment like this left out for easy plucking. We made a mistake. It happens."

I made a mistake, Ashe thought. Anger suddenly welled up within her, and she kicked the crate, swearing. "Of course . . . *of course* it was too good to be true." It wasn't so much the loss of money, though that certainly smarted. It was the loss of the chance to strike out at her parents' egos.

Ashe wilted, the anger draining from her as quickly as it had come.

Time was almost up. And the chances of finding and planning another major heist before her parents returned home was slim to nil. She'd wanted to end their spree with the biggest score yet. Instead, it was their worst. They were walking away from tonight with nothing.

"C'mon," said Jesse. "No use hanging around here. Let's head back to Lead Rose."

Ashe followed, silent, and they all climbed back on their bikes. As they headed back across the desert, the moon set, leaving the landscape around them as dark as Ashe's mood.

CHAPTER 14

Ashe always thought she'd wake up and feel different the day she turned eighteen. That there would be some palpable difference to the air, some special quality to the light, or a shift in the color of the sky. Logically, she knew that was silly; still, part of her couldn't help but expect it, especially now, when it meant life as she'd known it was about to change. But when the day did finally arrive, it started like most others had these last few months: with B.O.B. making breakfast, Frankie trying to reprogram the espresso machine to *finally* make it the way she liked it, and Julian stumbling downstairs sometime around noon.

And Ashe heading out to the barn to work on her chopper.

Usually, Jesse would accompany her, but today she slipped out on her own. Even if the world was the same, her place in it wasn't, and she needed some time to process that. The others must have sensed her need to be alone, because hours had passed and no one had come to look for her, not even B.O.B.

The world felt quiet as she ran a polishing cloth over the chopper's fresh candy-apple-red paint job. It shined with the sort of newness she thought she might have felt on this day, but instead, a cloud seemed to hang over her, refusing to leave. This was it—this was the day she was legally on her own. There'd been no happy birthday messages from her parents so far. Not that she'd expected any. They probably didn't even remember what day it was. But soon enough, they'd be back, and she'd be kicked out of Lead Rose.

Frustrated, Ashe let the polishing cloth fall. It wasn't only the significance of the date eating at her. No amount of work on the chopper, or anything else, over the past few days had succeeded in tamping down the anger and annoyance at the mistake they'd made in going after the crate of junk rifles. Worse was the fact that it had been *her* mistake.

She had been so *sure*.

"Hey, now." When she looked up, Jesse was leaning against the open barn door, the late-afternoon sun framing him. "No one should frown like that on their birthday."

"It's *my* birthday." Ashe tossed the cloth onto her workbench. "I'll frown if I want to."

"You're still upset about the other day."

It wasn't a question. And since it wasn't, Ashe didn't answer.

Jesse sighed and straightened. "Every lucky streak comes to an end, Ashe."

"Except we weren't depending on luck," said Ashe. "We had information, extensive planning—"

"And luck," he said. "It turned against us a bit, that's all. Anyway, what does it even matter now? Ashe—we're *loaded*. More money than any of us have ever seen, 'cept maybe you. And that's a result of your leadership. Forget one bad day. Especially on a day like today."

"I swear, Jesse McCree, if you tell me to smile—"

He grinned. "You'll punch me?"

"I'll punch you." Ashe gave him a look of challenge. "Would be fitting. I met you with a black eye. Maybe I'll leave you with one, too."

Jesse laughed. Despite her threat, he came over to where she worked, eyes tracing the lines of the chopper they'd spent so much time on. "Never thought that old wreck you hauled out of Trout's could look like this. What did you see in it back then anyway?"

Ashe warmed a little at the memory. "Honestly? Potential.

Which is all the four of us had then, and look at us now. This bike was there the day it all started. It's part of what we've built."

Jesse nodded. "Sure is. A 1976 classic . . . Hell, it'll probably last another eighty years and outlive every one of us. All that work, and now it's really done, huh?"

"Yeah, it's done."

It was a beauty, too. All the damage that had been done to it, all traces of its life as a loaner bike: gone. The red paint job ran from the extended nose all the way to the back, and three exhaust pipes angled up on either side of the body. It almost made the chopper look as if it had wings. And in a way, maybe it did—the bike was the first real piece of her new life, ready to carry her to wherever she wanted to go, and to whatever came next.

The thought was bittersweet. Finishing the hovercycle's refurbishment, turning eighteen—not so long ago those things had seemed far in the future. But now they were here, and Ashe still wasn't sure what was going to come next, any more than she had been on the day her parents disowned her.

"Hm . . . I don't know," said Jesse. "Don't get me wrong, that's a good-looking bike, but it doesn't look quite right yet. It's missing something."

Ashe's annoyance flared again. "What are you talking about? It's not missing anything. It's *perfect*."

"You sure?" Jesse reached into his pocket and pulled out a little black box, tied with a strip of white ribbon.

Confusion replaced Ashe's annoyance. "What's that?"

He tossed her the box. "Happy birthday, Ashe."

She caught it but, for a moment, all she could do was stare. "You . . . you got me something?"

"It's not a birthday without presents." Was it her imagination, or was he looking a little nervous? "Go on, open it."

She almost didn't want to, swimming pleasantly in the anticipation of doing so. It wasn't as if she hadn't gotten presents before. But the ones her parents had given her always seemed perfunctory, as if they were doing it mostly because that's what you did on a birthday or a holiday. Jesse's gift didn't strike her like that; there was real sincerity in the way he offered it to her.

Ashe slipped the bow off the box and pulled off the top. Inside, wrapped in a bit of tissue, was a key chain with her name on it. It was black metal except for the letters and the winged design below them, which shone rosy yellow.

For a moment, Ashe couldn't think of a single thing to say, not even thank you. "Is that gold?" she managed finally.

Jesse nodded. "In black steel. Didn't want you to forget where you came from, but also that it didn't need to be the only part of you. Maybe you've been as rich as gold, but you're tough as steel, too, Ashe."

She lifted the key chain from the box, letting it dangle between them. "I . . . don't know what to say. No, I do. Thank you. I love it." Her cheeks warmed as she looked up at him. "In fact, I think it might be the nicest thing anyone has ever given me."

"That's a shame," said Jesse, but there was no hint of teasing in the words.

She tapped the ignition switch on the hovercycle. "I was going to change the key ignition to a button one of these days, but I guess I'll leave it now. How charmingly old-fashioned."

Jesse smiled. "I think it's classic."

"You do, huh?"

Months ago, when she and Jesse were alone in the jail, she'd felt something—a strange kind of connection. And now that camaraderie felt stronger than ever, tested and tempered during their heists and over the hoverbike they'd worked so hard on together. Was that really going to be over in a few short days?

Ashe steeled herself. Yes, it was. That's what the agreement was. She had no right to ask for anything more than she already had.

Across from her, Jesse opened his mouth, as if to speak. But he didn't. There was an unseen boundary between them. What was on the other side, Ashe wasn't quite sure, but she did know one thing: She wasn't ready for what she had with Jesse—or Frankie and Julian—to be over yet.

And a part of her hoped that's exactly what Jesse McCree was thinking, too.

Suddenly, the sounds of metallic movement broke the spell. They both turned at the same time to find B.O.B. standing in the barn doorway, holding a bag. The omnic blinked at them.

Ashe stiffened, shoving the key chain back in the box, irritated at the flush that had risen to her cheeks. But the omnic was looking at Jesse. Was she mistaken, or did his eyes narrow slightly?

But Jesse didn't seem to notice. "Is it time?"

"Time for what?" said Ashe.

"We're taking you out to Cutthroat Trout's for your birthday." He went over to B.O.B. and took the bag. "Here."

Inside was her Calamity wig. She took it out, then hesitated, eyeing the chopper. "Don't you want to take her out for a test ride? You put in almost as much work as I did."

"C'mon," Jesse moved toward the door. "The bike will be there when we get back. Frankie and Julian have been looking forward to doing this all day."

He was right. Ashe had spent enough of this day alone. Jesse and B.O.B. waited as she put on her wig, then followed them back toward the manor. They didn't speak as they walked, but it was an easy, comfortable sort of silence. So much so that when they crested the last hill to the house, Ashe was nearly bowled over by the roar of sound that hit her.

"SURPRISE!"

For a moment, she didn't know what she was looking at. Jesse had said they were headed to Cutthroat Trout's, but it looked like Cutthroat Trout's had come to Lead Rose. Spread out on the patio outside the manor were dozens and dozens of people, smiling and raising their cups to her. Decorations peppered the manor as well—streamers and balloons and strings of colorful lights that pulsed in time with the music that suddenly began to play.

"What . . ." Ashe struggled to find her voice. "What is this?"

"It's a party," said Jesse. "You *have* been to a party before, right?"

"Of course, I have! Tons of them!" But this looked nothing like the parties her parents had thrown, full of business people, influential persons from Bellerae, whoever had managed to curry a drop of favor from them at the time. During those gatherings, Ashe had always kept to the fringes, generally ignored, unless her parents found a reason to drag her in front of one of their posh friends for a few minutes of awkward small talk.

Her hand flew to her wig suddenly. "Jesse, do they know about—?"

He shook his head. "They think we broke into the empty house to throw you a birthday bash."

Ashe relaxed. Her secret was safe. Even better was the cover story. Maybe she hadn't managed to embarrass her parents by intercepting an Arbalest prototype, but the idea of throwing a huge party in the manor without their permission was pretty satisfying. As Jesse led her down the hill, a warmth grew within her, seeing Lead Rose play host to a crowd unlike any it had seen before— racers and patrons from Cutthroat Trout's, friends and acquaintances from the local farms, even a few gang members (ones who didn't take offense from a little healthy competition).

And they were all here to celebrate her.

As they reached the patio, Frankie and Julian broke free of the crowd and came bounding over.

"There's the birthday girl!" Frankie carried one of the manor's countless crystal glasses. The drink sloshing around inside of it was nearly the same color as her lavender hair. "Well, what do you think?"

"You did all this?" said Ashe. "For me?"

"Of course!" said Frankie.

"It was a team effort." Julian glowed with excitement.

"Jesse and I decorated, Frankie wired up the lights, and B.O.B. cooked up a ton of treats."

"I love it," said Ashe. She felt like a damn fool as a grin spread across her face, but she wasn't able to keep it contained any longer. "I can't believe what y'all did in such a short time."

Jesse looked as satisfied as a cat that had gotten into the cream, but it was Frankie who looked confounded by Ashe's reaction.

"Did you really think we'd let your big day come and go without doing something?" the hacker asked.

Yes. But Ashe couldn't say that. How could she explain that she'd never had anyone in her life, besides B.O.B., who cared enough to do something like this for her? She looked around at Jesse, Frankie, and Julian, surer than ever that they were far more than her coconspirators—they were her *friends.* "I don't even know what to say."

"Say you're ready to have fun "—Frankie hooked an arm through Ashe's and dragged her deeper into the colorful fray—and let's get this party started!"

CHAPTER 15

By the time the sun set, Ashe had heard so many birthday well-wishes that she was beginning to feel dizzy with euphoria. Lead Rose Manor had turned into a world she'd never known before. Music pounded from all angles, and the halls buzzed with conversation and laughter. Everywhere Ashe went, people sat draped over the plush couches, or leaned against polished mahogany tables, sipping their drinks and enjoying the spread of snacks B.O.B. had cooked up. The energy of it was infectious. Even better, it would have made Ashe's parents *furious*.

That was the feeling that carried her through the rooms of the manor, head held high, a confident fire growing within her. No one here ignored her, or treated her like a doll to be taken out only on special occasions. In a few short months, Ashe had earned the esteem of a part of Bellerae she never knew existed, and it filled her with a sense of pride and purpose she hadn't been able to achieve before.

Too bad it'll all be over soon.

The thought was like being doused with a bucket of cold water. There was something bubbling up in Ashe, something she couldn't quite define. Tonight was energizing her in a way that the thought of leaving Bellerae never had. Maybe what she wanted wasn't out there, in the wide, unknown world.

Maybe it was right here.

But how? Ashe pushed the thought away, resolving to examine it more closely later. Right now, she was at the first party she'd ever been to that she actually liked, and she was going to *enjoy* it.

"Calamity!" Jaya, the announcer from Cutthroat Trout's, threw an arm around Ashe as she exited out onto the patio. She was as bright as a piece of candy in an electric-pink party dress, with matching lipstick. "What a perfect party! I can't believe that you managed to break into this place and throw it. Your little group really does have some skills." She raised her own glass of punch. "Everyone give a cheer for Calamity!"

Jaya didn't need Cutthroat Trout's sound system to get her voice to carry, and the air suddenly roared with ovations and merriment. Ashe drank them in. Maybe she should have felt embarrassed to be the center of attention when no one here except her own gang knew the truth of who she was—not Calamity, but Elizabeth Caledonia Ashe. But what kind of truth was that now, anyway? Jesse might have wanted to give their gang a name, but not having one didn't mean they were any less respected by the people now surrounding them.

And they were respected.

She was respected.

Ashe had lost Frankie a while ago—she seemed as comfortable flitting around the party as a butterfly around a meadow—but she spotted Jesse and Julian sitting on the periphery of the bustling patio, painted in a rainbow of colors by the lights dangling around them. Ashe made her way over to them, thankful for the rush of night air as she left the bulk of the crowd behind, cooling the excited warmth that seemed to have taken over her. Julian waved as she approached, grinning from ear to ear. Jesse smiled, too, but with more reserve.

Ashe flushed slightly again, feeling the weight of his gift in her pocket and thinking of their exchange in the barn earlier.

That thought she didn't set aside. Instead, she shoved it down as deep as it would go. No telling what would happen if she pulled on that thread. Her life was complicated enough right now. She wasn't going to lend a hand to complicating it further.

"Can't believe we waited so long to throw a party here," said Julian. "We should have been doing it all along. We could have been charging for this!"

Ashe laughed. "But then you would have had a lot less time to enjoy Lead Rose's charms *intact*."

Already, she'd noticed little things missing in the mansion—a paperweight here, a crystal bowl there. They'd made sure to lock down some rooms, like their bedrooms and the dining room, just in case anyone noticed a suspicious resemblance between the family portraits hanging there and the girl who called herself Calamity. At least there'd never been many photos of Ashe in the house to worry about. And as for the rest of her parents' stuff? Ashe couldn't have cared less. None of it meant anything to her, it was all just another hollow way her parents tried to show off their status.

"True," said Julian. "It has been fun playing rich. Maybe I'll keep on doing it."

"Hah," said Jesse, "like anyone would ever mistake you for some fancy aristocrat type. Then again"—he winked at

Ashe—"if 'Calamity' here can pass as gutter trash like us, I guess anything is possible."

She opened her mouth for a rebuke, but at that moment the music shifted again, a rousing beat rumbling across the patio.

Jaya appeared again, this time with Alyssa, who also worked at Trout's. They grabbed Ashe by the arms.

"Come dance with us!" said Jaya.

"Pleaaasse," pleaded Alyssa.

Ashe couldn't have refused even if she wanted, and she didn't. They dragged her onto the dance floor and there, surrounded by the new friends and community she'd finally found, Ashe gave herself over entirely to the intoxicating fun.

The thing about fun, though, was it had a way of making time go from a trickle to a rush. Before she knew it, hours had passed. Slowly but surely, the guests faded away, until Ashe could finally walk around the manor without being pulled aside constantly. She felt full and satisfied in a way she'd never experienced before. And it was all because of Jesse, Julian, and Frankie, who may have been the three people she saw least during the night. This was a celebration, and they should have been celebrating together—one another, and all the success they had managed over the last couple months.

Well, there was still time. But they should do it right.

Every year on her birthday, B.O.B. made a cake for her. It might only have been part of his programming at one point, but there was a part of her that had always appreciated the gesture and looked forward to it. Ashe made her way through the mansion to the kitchen, where she found exactly what she expected to find, hidden in the very back of the refrigerator: a triple-layer chocolate cake with chocolate frosting and an extra generous drizzle of chocolate glaze.

Her favorite.

She pulled it out of the fridge and placed it on the counter before rooting around in the drawers for a knife. One suddenly appeared in her peripheral vision. When she turned, she found B.O.B., offering up the implement.

"Thanks, B.O.B." Ashe took the knife. "The cake looks delicious." She started to rustle up some plates, too, then paused. Thanks to her parents' absence, she hadn't had many constants growing up—save for loneliness—but the omnic butler had always been there for her. Ashe looked up into his bright green optics. "You know I'm not letting Mom and Dad have you, right?" The words caught in her throat a little, even though B.O.B.'s expression remained as impassive as ever. "They don't deserve you. Wherever I go, you go with me, understand?"

"Well, isn't that touching."

Ashe and B.O.B. spun in unison at the sound of the new voice. Marco stood at the other end of the kitchen, flanked by Bez, Zeke, and three more of his most menacing-looking Diamondbacks. Ashe stepped backward, B.O.B. moving with her, as the gang leader slowly made his way across the room. He stopped by the cake, leaning on the counter as he dug a finger into the frosting and raised it to his mouth.

"Mm, that's good," he said.

Ashe glared at him. "What are you doing here?"

Marco arranged a look of mock sadness on his face. "I'm hurt, Ashe," he said. "You didn't invite us to your little party."

Anger flared as she began to respond, only to be quickly replaced by the cold sensation of fear. Her words caught in her throat.

Ashe.

Not Calamity, *Ashe*.

He'd called her by her real name.

"Oh, you get it now, huh?" Marco grinned triumphantly. "Did you really think that I was as dense or uninformed as the rest of the fools around here?"

Ashe's jaw tightened. "What do you want?"

"I warned you to stop those heists," said Marco. "And you ignored me outright. Shouldn't be a surprise, spoiled little rich girl like you. And since you couldn't end your spree on your own, I've come to tell you: I'm ending it for you."

Maybe she should have been afraid, but the smarmy, self-satisfied look on Marco's face sent a peal of laughter welling up in Ashe's chest. "Says *you*? I know you think you're tough because you're a big fish in a small pond, but guess what? That doesn't scare me in the least."

Marco smirked, unfazed. "You know, had this played out differently, I might have liked you, Ashe. You're smart, you're tough. Bez here even suggested you could have made a good addition to the Diamondbacks."

"Yeah, except I don't follow gutless pretenders who depend on bullying others to make themselves look like they're in control."

That bit deep. Marco's face twisted with rage for a moment. Sensing that, a couple of the Diamondbacks pulled out knives.

Ashe elbowed B.O.B. "Y'all sure you want to start something?"

The omnic straightened. The blades were useless against him, and in this confined space, he'd smash through the gang members like a wrecking ball.

"Marco . . ." said Bez, with a warning tone.

Marco ignored him, clearly still annoyed. "As much as you might deserve it, we didn't come here for a fight. We've already gotten everything we need tonight. Like I said, your fun is over, Ashe. I just wanted to make sure you knew who'd put an end to it." The satisfied grin returned. "We'll see ourselves out. Enjoy the rest of your little party."

With that, they filed out, leaving Ashe tense and bewildered. She'd expected a fight. A fight made sense from a meathead like Marco. But this? She stood in silence with B.O.B. for several minutes, letting her heartbeat return to normal. But a pit of something remained in her stomach.

With B.O.B. in tow, she headed through the mansion, keeping an eye out for the Diamondbacks as she did. But she didn't see any of them, just a few guests who were still lingering, sipping the dregs of their punch or yawning visibly. She found Frankie and Julian in the library.

"Did you see them?" Ashe demanded.

Frankie's brow furled. "See who?"

"Marco! The Diamondbacks were here."

Frankie and Julian traded a concerned glance.

"Why?" Frankie's voice was barely a whisper.

"Are they gone?" said Julian, at the same time.

"I think so, but I don't really know what they wanted." Words tumbled out of Ashe's mouth as she struggled to make sense of it. "It was confusing. I thought Marco was itching to throw down, but he just gave me another warning. He said he wanted to make sure I knew who put a stop to my fun, and that he's already gotten everything he needed and—"

There was a shattering of glass, and a bottle stuffed with a lit rag landed on the rug near them. Immediately, it burst into flames, spreading so fast that Julian had to vault over a sofa to escape it.

"What the hell?" cried Frankie.

A second window shattered as another bottle came flying in.

Ashe grabbed Frankie's arm. "C'mon! We need to get out of here."

"Are we under attack?" cried Julian.

"Unless this is your idea of a birthday surprise," said Ashe. "Move!"

She rushed them out back onto the patio as they heard more windows break in other parts of the mansion. By the time they got there, the mansion's fire suppressant system had kicked in, but the flames were still spreading. Smoke billowed from the library windows and half a dozen others. Guests poured out of every nearby exit, red-eyed and coughing.

"B.O.B.! Get back inside and make sure there's no one left."

The omnic obeyed, plunging into the dark smoke as Ashe looked around the patio. The few guests who were left were staring in shock at the chaos. Fortunately, no one appeared injured.

Then, suddenly, an icy feeling overcame Ashe. She looked

around again, more carefully this time, but without finding the face she was looking for. "Where's Jesse?"

"I don't know," said Frankie. "He was here not long ago, wasn't he?"

Julian shrugged.

Something in Ashe's chest tightened. "When was the last time either of you saw him?"

Frankie thought for a moment. "I–I don't know. A couple of hours?"

"It's been a while," said Julian.

"We have to find him," said Ashe. "Could he have taken his bike, gone riding?"

"Hold on." Frankie pulled out her tablet and began typing. A moment later, one of her microdrones launched from it, buzzing off in the direction of the barn.

Smoke poured from the mansion as they waited, but the flames began to subside, the fire suppression system starting to get ahead of them. After another long minute, B.O.B. came lumbering back outside.

"Did you find anyone?" Ashe said. "Did you see Jesse?" Slowly, the omnic shook his head. "Frankie?"

The hacker stared uneasily at the tablet. "He's not in the barn. And his bike is still there."

We've already gotten everything we need tonight. Cold

distress flooded Ashe as Marco's words came back to her in a rush. "The Diamondbacks took him." She knew it with sickening surety. "That's what Marco meant. That son of a—"

Suddenly, B.O.B. perked up like a hunting dog spotting game. A moment later, Ashe realized why.

Sirens.

She ran to the other end of the patio, where she could see the driveway that ran from the main road to the mansion. A dozen vehicles were tearing up it, sirens blaring and lights flashing. She'd know them anywhere: the Bellerae police.

"Of all the—who called *them*?" This was the last thing she needed right now. Ashe turned to the remaining guests. "Everybody go, now! Quickly!"

The guests scattered, running for their hoverbikes or other vehicles. The smart ones headed through the fields in the opposite direction of the approaching police force, but a few took their chances skirting around them. The gamble worked, as no one seemed inclined to pursue them.

"B.O.B., get inside and hide anything that might be incriminating. Frankie, Julian!" Ashe was nearly breathless with anxiety. Jesse was gone, kidnapped, and now there was this to deal with. "Get to the barn and hide. I'll take care of things here." How, she didn't know, but she was thankful that they hadn't kept any of their heist equipment in the mansion. "Pack up any evidence so we can move quickly and quietly if we need to. I'll meet you there later, when I can."

Without a word of argument, they nodded and took off, disappearing into the night only moments before the first of the police vehicles pulled up. Ashe started toward it, remembering at the last moment to pull her red Calamity wig off and toss it into a bush.

A party, she thought. *It was only a party that got out of hand. No one needs to know any more than that. Happens all the time. And this is still my hou—*

From the midst of the vehicles, a dark, familiar limousine appeared, and Ashe's stomach plunged into her boots.

A moment later, its doors opened, and out stepped her parents.

CHAPTER 16

If given the choice, Ashe would have strongly preferred to go up against Marco and every one of the Diamondbacks in that moment. Instead, she was face-to-face with her parents, and in those faces was a storm unlike anything Ashe had ever seen before. It was almost funny, in a way. The strings of colorful decorations combined with the clearing smoke and police lights just made them look as if they were guests of the party. It didn't help that the music was still playing, either, a wildly inappropriate background score for the scene that was unfolding.

Thankfully, a moment later, the music stopped. But it was already too late to do anything more to mitigate what her parents were seeing.

"Elizabeth Caledonia Ashe!" hissed her mother, overlapping her father's deeper growl of "What in the world is going on here?"

A few months ago, she might have shrunk back from their level of anger. But this time, it glanced off Ashe like a poorly timed slap. Because now it didn't matter. They'd already disowned her; what more could they do?

So Ashe stared squarely at her parents, and smiled. "Oh, you're back early. Shame, you just missed my birthday party."

"Birthday party?" her father sputtered. "Is that what this chaos is? Look what you've done to our house. Who gave you permission to have a party?"

"No one," Ashe threw back, crossing her arms. "I'm eighteen today, remember? I don't need your permission anymore."

Sheriff Carson appeared behind her parents, looking more fed up than she'd ever seen before. "Like I said, Mr. and Mrs. Ashe. We got an anonymous tip that some hooligans had broken into your estate. Looks like that wasn't quite the whole story. I should have guessed."

Ashe laughed and wheeled on her parents. "You two seriously dropped everything and flew all the way back here because of a *party*? Was your business going so poorly? Or could you simply not stand the thought of me having fun?"

"Our *business* is exactly why we came home early." There was ice in her mother's tone. "The sheriff simply caught us en route, and met us at the airstrip. The real reason we're here has to do with a recent string of robberies of Arbalest cargo."

The way she said it made something in Ashe's stomach clench.

"We'd thought they were just an uptick in the deviant gang activity around Bellerae," her mother continued, "but your father and I *also* got a tip. One that made us look a little closer at some of the circumstances surrounding the robberies." She moved closer to Ashe, like a snake slithering closer to its prey. "There were some . . . consistencies. But we weren't sure until a few days ago, when someone stole a shipment of old Arbalest rifles that were slated for recycling. At least, that's how they were listed everywhere but one: in our personal administrative accounts. And then we saw where those files were being accessed from."

Most of Ashe's earlier bravado drained away. But not all of it. Her parents knew; she understood that. That didn't mean she needed to give them the satisfaction of a confession. "And where was that?"

Her mother's eyes narrowed. "How could you, Elizabeth? Stealing from your own family?"

"*My family?*" Ashe gritted her teeth, anger rising like a tide within her. "You mean the one who disowned me as of today, who were going to kick me out with nowhere to go, all because of a fight I didn't even start? You mean *that* family?"

Ashe's father had the grace to look slightly embarrassed, eyes glancing around at the sheriff and other police officers. Not that it meant much; the shame wasn't about what he'd done, only that he'd been caught doing it.

But her mother didn't flinch, or look away from her. "Oh honestly, Elizabeth," she said, sounding exasperated, "did you really believe we were going to disown you? Our only child?"

Ashe blinked at her parents, utterly bewildered.

"You were out of control," her father continued. "You needed to be taught a lesson. Yes, it was a drastic step to make you think we were going to cut you off, but *something* needed to be done to convince you to clean up your act!"

The world seemed to warp around Ashe, twisting in some way she couldn't comprehend. Were they telling the truth? Or was this simply a performance, a rewriting of the punishment they'd threatened, in order for her parents to save face in front of Bellerae's police force?

Something needed to be done.

You needed to be taught a lesson.

It didn't matter. Ashe drew in a deep breath and stood straighter. The truth wasn't important, not now. She'd never been out of control. She simply wasn't the complacent, obedient follower her parents had always wanted.

And she never would be.

The past few months had taught her that much about herself. She looked around at the Bellerae police, at the still-smoking mansion, and at her parents, with the carefully curated image that they were desperate to maintain. These were the pieces of her old life.

A life she didn't want anymore.

"It doesn't matter," Ashe said aloud. "I'm done—with all of this, and with both of you. I don't need any of it anymore."

Her mother looked surprised, but only for a moment. Then her eyes went hard. "You know, Elizabeth, I used to think you were misguided, a little too spirited for your own good. I thought having to confront the idea of being on your own would be to your benefit. But now I know better: At your core, you're nothing more than a base, common criminal."

"Strange," said Ashe, glaring right back. "I would have

thought that made me the perfect candidate to work with you and all those corporate buddies whose boots you line up to lick."

Her mother's hand flickered up, as if she was about to slap Ashe, but it stopped halfway. "Sheriff," she called instead. "Get over here."

Looking a bit sour about being ordered around, Sheriff Carson nonetheless came hustling to Ashe's mother's side. "Ma'am?"

"Arrest her." There was no affection left in her mother's eyes, no hint of parental familiarity. "Like Elizabeth said, she's eighteen now, so she can't dodge the responsibility of her actions any longer. I want her thrown in jail. We'll see to it she's brought up on every charge we can find." Her mother turned away.

"No!" The Diamondbacks had Jesse. She needed to get away from this mess and find a way to help him. But it was no good. A pair of deputies had flanked her during the argument, and they grabbed her arms when she made a move to run.

But her mother ignored her objection. "Maybe being locked up for real will finally teach you a lesson, Elizabeth."

Ashe stopped fighting as the deputies dragged her across the lawn toward their vehicles. "I hope you remember this," she called back to her parents, letting all the bitterness she felt leech into her voice. "Because I know I won't forget."

It was almost funny, being back in the cell that started it all. Except there was no room left in Ashe for *funny* right now. What did fill her was a smothering slurry of anger, embarrassment, and fear—for Jesse, not for herself. She kept looking over at the cell beside hers, half expecting him to be there, feeling a part of her flake away every time she glimpsed the empty bench. What were the Diamondbacks doing to him? It was clear that Marco had been the one to tip off her parents and the cops about the party, and then set the fire as a little extra jab, but then why take McCree?

For hours, she flipped the questions over in her head like a coin, but one that always landed in an unclear way. Marco must have expected for her to get off with a scolding from her parents, since it was her house, after all. Was McCree some kind of insurance? For what, she wasn't sure, but that was going to be the first problem she tackled the moment she got out of here.

And how had Marco known who she was in the first place? Another question that continued to vex her. They'd been so careful, and no one had seemed to see through her Calamity disguise before.

It didn't matter. What did was getting out and getting to the others, so they could rescue Jesse.

"Sheriff! Sheriff!"

She'd spent a good hour yelling when he'd first thrown her in here, not to mention the hell she'd raised the whole ride from the mansion. It hadn't worked then, and she didn't expect it to work now. But it was all she could think of. So, no one was more surprised than she was when the sheriff appeared in the hall, approaching her with a thoroughly fed-up look on his face.

"It didn't need to be like this, Elizabeth," he said with no lack of disappointment and annoyance. "But you've really done it now. Starting a gang? Stealing from your family's company? With the number of charges you're about to be slapped with, you're going away until you have the wrinkles to match that white hair of yours."

She clenched the bars in her fists. "Oh yeah? Where's the proof?"

They'd sold everything they'd stolen, and the transactions were untraceable. Frankie had made sure of that. And even if they found the barn, there wouldn't be much more than a bunch of hoverbikes and computer parts by this point.

Not exactly incriminating of anything more than having an engrossing hobby, and a few new friends. Sure, maybe her parents knew Ashe had been accessing their files, but who was to say she'd done anything other than look? The party was another matter, and the fire, but was a court of law really going to waste much time on a birthday celebration that had gotten out of hand?

The sheriff sighed. "You and I both know that with parents like yours, and all of their resources, it won't matter. No one is going to get the charges against you dropped this time, Ashe. From what they said, it sounds more like they're going to do whatever they can to make them stick."

He was right. It grated Ashe to admit it, but that was exactly what was going to happen. "Look, I can't stay here. I have a friend, he's in trouble, and if I don't get out of here—"

"You think I'm going to open the door and let you waltz out because of a friend?"

"No," Ashe replied, increasingly infuriated. "But my parents don't get to change how the whole system of law works, do they? The court's already set my bail by now, right?"

The sheriff looked at her skeptically. "Sure, but how would you pay it? It's not exactly pocket change, and I doubt any of your lines of credit are working now."

"I don't need my parents' money anymore. I have my own now. A lot of it."

At that, the sheriff laughed. "And how did you get that, I wonder? Careful, Elizabeth; you're getting close to an admission of guilt."

It didn't matter that he knew the money was the result of her heists. Now he knew she had it. She could work with that. "I haven't admitted to anything, Sheriff. Save that I have an account that could be called upon to pay my bail."

"Forget it"—he shook his head—"I don't need the wrath of the Ashe family."

"No, but you're the one who always complained about us getting what we wanted, because of who we were." Ashe chose her words carefully. "Well, you heard my parents, Sheriff. They've disowned me for real. I'm not part of the family anymore."

The sheriff said nothing, but he eyed her more closely.

"You want to see my parents knocked down a few pegs?" she continued. "Let me pay my bail. I've got the account numbers and all the right codes. Nothing would make them angrier than me walking out of here, and them not being able to do a damn thing about it."

Oh, he was mulling it over. She could see it on his face, plain as day.

"C'mon, Sheriff," she pushed. "Aren't you as tired of playing by their rules as I am?"

His expression turned skeptical. "What guarantee would I have that, once you posted bail, you'd show up to court when called?"

That made her smile. "None at all." He didn't look surprised by the reply. "Look, I know you and I don't exactly have the nicest history between us. But I'm not going to lie to you, not about this. I know two things: One, that as soon as I get out of here, I'm going after my friend; and two, I'm done with my parents. Like they said, I'm eighteen now. That means neither of us need to get their permission when it comes to my bail. You've always hated their sway, all because . . . What did you say? Because they own half the town? Well, Sheriff, do they own *you*?"

Less than an hour later, she was free. And poor, once again. Her bail, covering the many crimes she was accused of, had been astronomical—taking almost everything there was in the gang's shared account. That had left a feeling like a hole in her gut, but it was nothing compared to the one eating deeper and deeper as the minutes ticked by and the Diamondbacks still had Jesse. And yet, she couldn't help but reflect on how her parents' interference had left her exactly where they had intended—eighteen, penniless, and without anywhere to call home.

But even if her blood relations had cast her aside, Ashe had found a new family to take their place.

And one of those people was in trouble.

That was the thought in the front of her mind as she burst through the front doors of the police station. It receded only briefly when she saw who was waiting outside: B.O.B., dripping with rain, even though he held an umbrella. He must have been waiting for hours.

As worried as she was about Jesse, for a moment, she froze, held in place by more emotions than she was used to, and far more than she liked.

B.O.B. blinked at her.

Ashe looked around. The street was empty. Then she went to the omnic, throwing her arms around him, never mind that he was soaked through. She said nothing, and didn't need to, as B.O.B. put a hand on her shoulder. Maybe he wasn't the most talkative omnic out there, but when it came down to it, he was loyal to Ashe. And she was loyal to him. In this new life of hers, B.O.B. was family, too.

"C'mon," she said finally, wiping away what, if anyone had asked, she would have sworn up and down were raindrops. "And send a message to Frankie. Make sure she and Julian made it to the barn, and tell them I'll meet them there in a little bit. We've got work to do."

I'm coming to save you, Jesse, she thought as they started back toward Lead Rose, *and I'll bring hell with me, if that's what it takes.*

CHAPTER 17

There was one stop Ashe needed to make first. It wasn't the smartest one, maybe, but it needed to be done. She needed to close the last door on her old life. And that meant she needed to return to the scene of the crime.

It was strange, to see Lead Rose so silent after, only a few hours before, its halls had hosted such liveliness. Now, as Ashe crept through its grounds, it was more like approaching a mausoleum, albeit one that was slightly singed by recent arson. B.O.B.'s interface with the house meant any security measure that might have alerted someone to her presence was disabled, but Ashe didn't see any signs of life as she approached.

"Anyone home, B.O.B.?" Hidden behind a hedge, they were close enough for her to see the remnants of the birthday party gone bad. Abandoned cups and plates, leftover snack foods, and the lingering smell of burnt oil and flame-retardant chemicals.

The omnic went still for a moment, then shook his head.

Ashe wasn't surprised. Even though their bedrooms were nowhere near where the fire had been, her parents hadn't deigned to stay in the damaged house. They were probably fast asleep in the penthouse of the best hotel in town. Which was fine. She'd promised them that they'd never see her again, and she meant it. Still, Ashe kept quiet as B.O.B. unlocked a door, slipping inside like she was just another shadow. The last few months had been the first time in years she'd been happy in this house. Now she was walking its halls for what was likely the final time.

The thought didn't bother her half as much as she might have expected.

Immediately, she headed upstairs to the bedrooms. The doors to where Frankie, Julian, and Jesse had been sleeping were open, their stuff gone from sight. B.O.B. had thankfully done a thorough job of hiding anything that might be incriminating, including their presence in the manor. Continuing on to her room, Ashe went inside and grabbed a backpack. She ignored her tablet and other electronics—anything Arbalest might be able to track—packing only some clothing and a few personal items. Everything else, she was happy to abandon. It wasn't her, not anymore. In the end, the entirety of her life at Lead Rose Manor came to less than half a rucksack.

"B.O.B., go grab the others' things." Ashe closed up her bag, then headed back downstairs. Already, she'd begun to itch, being here. She didn't want to be in this place a minute longer than she needed to.

But as she passed the dining room, she paused, suddenly pensive. The doors were still closed and locked. Ashe keyed in the code to open them, entering to find the room awash in the murky light of dawn. In the dining room, the portrait of her great-great-great-grandmother seemed as austere as ever, but it was the white envelope on the mantel opposite the portrait that drew Ashe's eye. It was the card her parents had sent the morning of her graduation, right where she'd left it months ago. How different might things be now if only they hadn't left? Would Ashe be sound asleep upstairs, left alone yet again? Or was it possible she'd be thousands of miles away, shadowing her parents as they tried to impose on her the tricks of their trade?

There was no way to know. But what was certain was, if her

parents had kept their promise, she never would have met Jesse, or Julian, or Frankie. And that opened a bigger hole in her than the thought of never seeing Lead Rose again.

This was no longer her home. Arbalest was no longer her company. And her parents were no longer her family. She might still be Elizabeth Caledonia Ashe, but she'd become a version of herself that no one could have possibly predicted.

Ashe's gaze fell to the Viper rifle, and a warm feeling suddenly swelled in her chest. But it wasn't nostalgia. It was the thought of the Ashe family legacy, and how she didn't have to leave the entirety of it behind. How there was one piece that she could take with her, and one that she, more than anyone else, deserved.

Ashe grabbed the Viper and walked out the dining room door.

The barn was haloed in dawn's light by the time Ashe got there, B.O.B. trailing silently behind her. It was quiet when she approached, but she knew she wasn't alone as soon as she spotted what looked like a big fly buzzing around the entrance. Moments later, the barn door flew open and out rushed Frankie, followed by a pale, hollow-eyed Julian.

"Ashe!" Frankie's features were tight with concern. "What

happened? We hid and watched the sheriff take you away, but then B.O.B. sent me a message and—"

"I got out," said Ashe simply. "The sheriff let me post my bail. Remind me to send him a nice card when all this is over."

"He let you—" Frankie stopped. "Wait, how did you pay for it?"

Ashe looked away. It wasn't that she regretted what she'd done, but she also hadn't been looking forward to telling the others about it. "I used our shared account."

Frankie's brow furrowed. "How much?"

"Almost all of it. But I didn't have a choice."

"What?" Julian's mouth dropped open. "You blew our *whole* account?"

"*Most*, not all," Ashe repeated. There wasn't time for this. "We earned it once; we can earn it again. Right now, we need to work on a plan."

"A plan for what?" said Frankie, still looking shocked.

"What do you mean, *for what*?" Ashe pushed by them and into the barn, tossing her bag into a corner. The bikes were untouched where they had left them, further confirmation neither her parents nor their lackeys had discovered their hideout. "The Diamondbacks took Jesse! We need to get him back!"

Frankie and Julian traded a troubled look.

"C'mon," Ashe ordered, grabbing her Seraphim rifle and

Jesse's spare revolver from the rack on the wall. "Gimme some ideas. There must be some way to figure out where they've taken him."

"Don't need to," Frankie said distantly, as if only half listening to what Ashe said. "I know exactly where they'll go—their hideout in the old Route 66 rest area over near Deadlock Gorge. But there's no way we're getting in there without them knowing. And even if we do, the chances of getting out alive are a million to one."

"That's not zero," said Ashe, continuing her preparations. "And we have an advantage—you used to run with them, so you know the hideout, right? What kind of security does it have? What's the best way to hit them so that they won't see us coming?"

Silence filled the barn.

Ashe turned back to the pair, waiting for an answer. "Well?"

Frankie opened her mouth to speak, stopped, and then sighed. "Ashe, what are you thinking? The Diamondbacks outnumber us five times over. There's no way we're going to be able to go up against them and then walk away, much less rescue Jesse."

"We will and we can," Ashe insisted. "We just need a good plan. It doesn't matter what the Diamondbacks have in numbers, they can't even begin to match us in brains.

Marco, especially. That lunkhead is going to find out what happens when he crosses me or mine."

Still, Julian looked unsure. "I don't know, Ashe. Maybe we should wait a bit, think this through."

"Ashe, I need you to listen to me," said Frankie, taking her by the shoulders. "This is madness. You want to go in there, guns blazing, but I'm telling you the truth: That's going to get us all killed. *Really killed*."

A sour taste filled Ashe's mouth. "Are you saying we should do nothing? Give up on Jesse?"

"No." Frankie let out an exasperated breath. "It's only . . . You don't understand. Marco isn't the forgiving type. Better to wait until he gives you a chance to do something in return for Jesse, like pay a ransom."

"Exactly," said Julian, brightening a little.

"Pay a ransom with what?" Ashe felt the heat rise in her cheeks. "How much do you two have left in your personal accounts? Because mine is dry. And what would I be able to do in exchange for Jesse? The only thing Marco might want from me is information about Arbalest, and I don't have access to those files anymore. I've got this"—she tapped her temple—"and I've got this." She hefted the Viper rifle. "And even if that's all I've got, that's what I'm going to use to save Jesse."

Frankie's lips thinned. "Then you're both gonna end up in an early grave."

Ashe gritted her teeth. "Not if we work together. But it sounds like you have no plans to do that. Do you even care that they took Jesse, Frankie? Or do your old friends suddenly look a whole lot better than your current ones?"

The hacker scowled. "That's not fair."

"Isn't it? I thought all these months together meant something. That the four of us"—Ashe glanced at B.O.B—"the *five* of us had put together a real team. Not too long ago, the sky was the limit so long as we worked together. But now one of us is in trouble, real trouble, and you're ready to turn tail and abandon him."

"That's not true!" Frankie yelled. "You don't think I'd get Jesse back in a heartbeat if I could? And don't talk to me about what this was. We worked our butts off on those heists, only for you to go and blow our earnings on getting yourself out of jail. You didn't ask us for help first, or for permission, you just went ahead and did it."

Ashe started to speak but Frankie kept going.

"Because it's nothing to you, is it, 'boss'?" The word dripped with venom. "There's always more money to be made for types like you. You say what we did means something to you, but is it any more than a game? Any more than what your parents are always doing with their elite corporate friends? I had plans for that money, Ashe. Plans to help my family and friends back home. And now those plans are dead in the water because of something *you* decided, on your own. How can you call us a team and then make a decision like that?" Frankie turned away, fists clenched. "From the moment we started this, you were always the one with the least to lose."

For a moment, Ashe couldn't speak. Her blood pulsed with anger and frustration, mouth open but empty of words. How could Frankie be mad? She'd used the money to bail herself out of jail because of Jesse. *For* Jesse. She would have done the exact same thing for any of them.

"Fine," Ashe spat finally. "If that's how you feel, you don't need to be a part of this anymore." Ashe turned to Julian. He'd kept quiet during their argument, but straightened the moment Ashe's gaze fell on him, looking like a mouse who'd been spotted by a snake. "Julian, you're with me, right?"

Julian said nothing for a moment, then wagged his head up and down. "Of course. Ashe. I'm with you one hundred percent. Find the Diamondbacks, save Jesse, ride into the sunset—all that."

"Good." Ashe grabbed Jesse's rifle and tossed it to him. "B.O.B., you hold on to the Viper." She handed the antique weapon to the omnic. "It's not what we'll need for a firefight like this, but it won't hurt to have along. Grab anything else we've got left, too, and load it onto the bikes—ammo, explosives, even those junk rifles from the last heist. EVERYTHING."

B.O.B. nodded.

"Then let's go." Ashe pointedly threw a nasty look at Frankie and climbed onto her chopper. "Jesse needs us. He's one of our gang. He's *family*. And I'll be damned if we're going to let him down."

CHAPTER 18

Deadlock Gorge was not the sort of place nice young ladies from Bellerae went, so Ashe had seen it only in pictures. Oh, she knew it was popular at one time, that hundreds of thousands of tourists used to traverse old Route 66, which cut through the gorge. Once, Deadlock Gorge had been a destination, a place for tourists to stop and enjoy the view, followed by a meal at the delightfully kitschy Panorama Diner.

Now it was the sort of place you visited at your own risk, run for all intents and purposes by the Diamondbacks.

Ashe had to admit, it wasn't a bad place for a hideout. Far enough from Bellerae that the law left them alone, but close enough to make trouble, when trouble needed to be made.

And this, Frankie had said, was where they had brought Jesse.

From a distance, it didn't look like much. Ashe, Julian, and B.O.B. hid on the top of a ridge, looking down to where a few hoverbikes sat parked outside the High Side Cantina. The watering hole looked much like everything else in the rest area did these days, run-down and practically abandoned. When they'd passed the Panorama Diner earlier, barely a handful of patrons were visible through the windows, and Ashe wasn't even sure the gas station was open. But none of that was what mattered. What did was the pair of metal doors set into the wall of the canyon, tucked behind the cantina. That was it, she knew immediately—the entrance to the Diamondbacks' hideout. There were some other possible entrances—tunnels boarded up here and there— but it was clear that the doors were the main way in. And probably the best way out.

Ashe was no fool; she'd heard what Frankie had said. Attacking the hideout head on was a bad idea added to an already bad situation. But Jesse was inside, which meant she needed to get the Diamondbacks outside.

"You solid on what to do?" Ashe lowered her field glasses and turned to Julian.

He looked nervous, but nodded, holding up a small, handheld detonator. "I'm the distraction."

They both looked over at the crate of dynamite strapped to the back of Julian's bike. It was more than a little old-fashioned, but after the failed rail-stop heist, they'd been almost out of explosive charges. This was all they could find at the last minute, and even these had taken the dregs of what remained in their shared account to buy from Fort Starr.

The dynamite bundles were ready to go. All Julian needed to do was place them in strategic places and then detonate them. With any hope, the chaos would draw the Diamondbacks out and give Ashe an opening to sneak in. She knew not all of the rats would be flushed out, but anything they could do to even up the numbers for her offensive would help.

"I'm gonna need all the time I can get," said Ashe, "so make sure that distraction is as big as possible. B.O.B., you stay up here until the fireworks start. It'll be easier for you to sneak down after that. And once you do get near the hideout entrance, keep out of sight. I'll give you a call if I need help."

The omnic gave her a thumbs-up.

"Okay." Ashe shouldered her rifle and straightened her hat. No wig anymore, her white hair was out for all to see, though she'd braided it to keep it out of the way. Calamity was nothing more than a piece of her now; she had no illusions that Marco had kept her secret. Chances were, anyone who'd known her by her other persona now knew who she really was, or would know soon enough. Though, honestly, it was a relief to be done with the fiction, in the same way it was a relief to be done with her old life. "Give me a few minutes to get down the ridge. I'll find a spot to hunker down behind the cantina. Let me know when you're ready to make some noise."

Julian looked nervous, but he climbed onto his bike. "Right. See you down there."

He sped off without another word.

Ashe gave B.O.B. a quick pat, then started to make her way down into the gorge, following paths that looked like they'd been cut into the stone way back when Arbalest had been founded. She kept back from the edge so as to stay out of sight, but there were so few people around she needn't have bothered. She reached the floor of the canyon and slipped around the side of the cantina, crouching behind a stack of discarded tires and rusty vehicle parts.

There, she checked her rifle, making sure for the hundredth time it was fully loaded and the sight clean. It felt different, going up against real people instead of drones. But what other choice did she have now? She didn't want to hurt anyone if it could be helped, but at the same time, nothing—and no one—was going to stop her from rescuing Jesse.

"I'm ready, Julian," she whispered.

No answer. But that didn't mean anything. Julian would be keeping out of sight, too, as he set the dynamite charges. Maybe he didn't want to alert anyone to his presence by making noise. Right now, patience was the name of the game.

So, Ashe waited. And waited. Minutes ticked by, and with each one Ashe's palms grew a little sweatier and her heart beat a little harder. It was the adrenaline of the job, taking hold of her. She couldn't have fought it if she wanted to. She was ready to go.

But still, there were no explosions.

"Julian?" she whispered again. "What are you doing out there, taking a nap?" Still nothing. Were the walls of the canyon interfering with the signal? No, Frankie had designed their communication tech, and that's something she would have accounted for. "Julian, say something!"

"Sorry . . ." A shadow fell over Ashe. "He won't be answering to you anymore."

She looked up to see Marco grinning down at her. Ashe swung the rifle around for a desperate shot, but Marco grabbed the barrel and yanked it away, right as two more

Diamondbacks appeared and grabbed hold of her. She screeched as she lost her grip on the gun, and kicked out at Marco, but it was no good. A cloth bag descended over her head, turning the whole world gray. A moment later there was a violent, stinging pain in her side.

Then nothing.

Ashe awoke somewhere very different. She knew that immediately. In the gorge, she'd been able to feel the sun, and the warmth radiated by the surrounding walls of stone. She'd been able to smell the hints of gasoline and old fryer oil in the air. But here—wherever that was—felt far cooler, with a slight hint of mildew. Or maybe that was just the bag that was still over her head.

She was lying on her side, arms aching like fire. But when she tried to move them, she couldn't. Some kind of restraints bound her wrists.

She groaned.

Nearby, something shuffled.

"There you are."

It was Marco. She'd know his arrogant tone of voice anywhere. A moment later, the bag over her head was yanked off. Ashe lay on the cement floor in some kind of cavern turned warehouse and loading dock, Marco grinning his stupid seedy grin over her.

"Hey, Ashe," the gang leader said. "Have a nice nap?"

Enraged, she strained against her restraints again, feeling the bite of metal into her flesh.

Bez stood beside him, holding the bag they'd blindfolded her with. "You might as well stop fighting," he said. "You're only going to make this worse."

"What the hell did you do to me?" Ashe spat on the floor, mouth tasting like she'd been sucking on copper pennies.

Marco held up a taser. "Just a little love tap. You're fine, rich girl. In fact, you're lucky that's all you got. No telling what we might have done to you if we hadn't known you were coming."

Ashe started. "What?"

"Oh, don't look so surprised." Marco gave a little snort of laugher. "Do you really think everyone you meet falls in line behind you like an obedient little sheep? That they don't keep their eyes open for a better deal? Awful shortsighted of you, Ashe."

Ashe felt a chill rippling down her spine. They'd known she was coming. They'd known right where to find her. The cold turned to a hot flush of rage as she strained against the metal cuffs that bound her. Someone had ratted her out to the Diamondbacks.

And there was only one possibility: *Frankie*.

She gritted her teeth, regretting forever having caught sight of the hacker's file. Sure, Frankie had been against trying to save Jesse. And she'd been mad at Ashe for using their money to bail herself out. But Ashe had thought Frankie was a friend. A *real* friend. But she'd turned on the gang as soon as things came a little undone. Loyalty had never been her strong suit, right from the beginning. She'd said it herself; she was a freelancer. And freelancers went to the highest bidder.

"Where's Jesse?" Had they gotten Julian, too? Ashe didn't ask, in case they hadn't and he'd gotten away, or was still out there. That gave her hope. She may be in the Diamondbacks' clutches, but not far away was one big, tough omnic butler and a kid with an entire crate of dynamite.

"He's safe," said Bez.

"For now," Marco added.

"I don't believe you." She looked around, scanning the loading dock for any sign of Jesse. From her vantage point, she couldn't see the metal doors that led outside to the gorge, but they couldn't be far. What she could see were crates lining the walls, piled almost to the ceiling, a large, open shipping container, and, off to one side, a handful of hoverbikes—

Her stomach tightened. One of the bikes was familiar. No,

not only familiar—she'd know it anywhere. After all, she'd seen it only a little while ago, with the same crate lashed to the back.

"Well"—Marco shrugged—"then maybe you'll believe *him*."

At the same moment Ashe realized who the bike belonged to, Julian slid into view.

CHAPTER 19

So much for family. For loyalty. For friendship.

"You?" Whatever flashed on Ashe's face, it was enough for Julian to take a sudden, scared step back. "You're the one who sold me out?"

He gave her a sheepish look, freckled cheeks reddening. "Sorry, Ashe. It was never personal."

First Frankie, now Julian. After all they'd done together, none of it had mattered in the end. How could Ashe have been so foolish to trust so many traitors? She lay on the floor, seething with anger and helpless to do anything about it, and upset that she was so helpless in the first place.

"It was great working with you and all," Julian continued,

"but we knew from the beginning it wasn't going to last forever. And you should have stopped when Marco told you to. But you didn't and, well . . ." He hesitated for a moment, scratching at the back of his neck self-consciously. "You know all those nights at Trout's? Turns out my run of bad luck is more of a marathon. I got in deep with a few folks that weren't going to take an IOU."

Zeke came into Ashe's view, along with some of the other Diamondbacks. He let out a loud laugh. "Deep? Kid, you'd dug a grave for yourself. You're lucky we came along when we did."

Ashe's jaw tightened. "What does he mean by that?"

"Well," said Julian, reluctantly, "Marco made me a good offer to help pay off my debts."

"It *was* a great offer," Marco said sourly. "Julian had already told us all we wanted to know about you and your operation—right down to who you really were. He even suggested we get McCree in on a little scheme—offering him a place in the Diamondbacks at your party and then pretending to ransom him to you in exchange for the profits from your heists. They'd still get their cut, and we'd get the rest. Too bad McCree isn't as smart as Julian here, and that he tried to warn you about what we were up to." He shrugged. "But willing participant or not, the plan was the same. At least until you threw a wrench into it."

"You can't blame that on me!" stammered Julian. "There was no way I could have known she'd use all our money to get herself out of jail!"

Marco's gaze snapped to him. "Don't tell me what I can and can't blame you for. You're just lucky Little Miss Arbalest decided to come after McCree. Now she can be the one we ransom, and her moneybags parents can foot the bill."

For the first time, Ashe felt like smiling. It was a grim smile, but a smile nonetheless. "*That's* what you're planning to do? Ransom me to my parents? Hope the number you have in mind is a big, round zero, because that's all they'll be willing to pay for me these days."

Marco sighed, clearly unconvinced. "Yes, yes, you've had your little tiff with Mummy and Daddy. And maybe they don't think you're worth the lint in their pockets. But does the rest of the world know that? They have a reputation to maintain, after all. And as soon as the *Daily Pioneer* gets wind that you're being held for ransom—and you can bet they'll get tipped off quickly—your parents will pay whatever I want simply to avoid the embarrassment."

"Maybe." Ashe had to admit, it was sound enough reasoning. The kidnapping of an heiress was the kind of juicy scandal the paper loved, and it would be even juicier if it was *her.* "But I wouldn't lay a big bet on that. For all you know, they'll spill the beans on their thief of a daughter, make it look like a scam we're in on together. That's how I'd spin it, if I were them. And even if they do pay for my return, I hope you have a plan to run for the hills immediately, because if I have the chance to get my hands on you—"

"You'll what?" said Marco. "You talk awfully tough for someone trussed up like a turkey."

The Diamondbacks laughed. Julian, wisely enough, didn't join in.

It should have sent a fresh rush of rage through her. But Ashe, apparently, had hit her limit on anger. Instead, her focus turned cool and sharp, like when she was lining up a shot with her rifle. Her friends were either prisoners or had abandoned her. She was unarmed. And even B.O.B. wouldn't be able to take on the whole Diamondback gang, even if she'd had a way to alert him.

But that didn't mean she was about to give up.

"Bez, you and Julian toss her into the cell with her little friend," ordered Marco. Then he sneered at Ashe. "Sorry it's not the sort of accommodations you're used to, milady."

"He's so full of hot air, isn't he?"

Ashe stiffened at the voice that came out of nowhere. *Frankie?*

A moment later she felt the telltale tickle behind her ear as one of Frankie's microdrones latched on.

"But if there's one thing about Marco, it's that he's

predictable. For example, I didn't need to use my microdrones to know he'd use digitally-locked manacles on you instead of good, old-fashioned rope."

There was a *click,* and Ashe felt the pressure around her wrists lessen.

"Be ready."

Ready? Ashe searched the warehouse as inconspicuously as she could while Julian hesitantly circled behind her, and started to pull her to her feet. *Ready for what?*

Suddenly, sirens blared in the distance.

Julian released her as Marco and the others spun in the direction of the doors to the gorge.

"What in the world is that?" Marco cried.

"Bellerae police!" came an amplified voice that echoed through the cavern. "Throw down your weapons and come out with your hands where we can see them!"

"Police?" Marco swore. "How did they find us?"

Clang! The sound echoed through the cavern. *Clang!*

"I don't know," said Bez. "But they're trying to break down the doors!"

Clang! Clang! CLUNK.

Ashe smiled at the distinct sound of a very large piece of metal hitting a concrete floor. "Looks like you should have been more careful, Marco. How much prison time do you think you'll get for kidnapping the Arbalest heiress?"

Marco glared at her a moment, then turned to the gang. "Scatter!"

The Diamondback leader headed into a side tunnel, the other gang members on his heels. Julian tried to follow, but Ashe kicked out, tripping him. He went sprawling.

"Oh no you don't, traitor!" She pulled off the manacles and lunged for Julian, twisting his arms around his back as she clamped the restraints onto him. "You're not going anywhere."

"Ashe, wait . . ." he pleaded.

"Shut up!" she cried as footsteps approached from the direction of the doors.

But they weren't sound of normal footsteps. No, she'd know that heavy tread anywhere.

"B.O.B.!" Ashe swelled with excitement as the omnic rounded the bend and came running into the warehouse. He slowed as he reached her, one of the Seraphim rifles slung over his shoulder, along with the Viper she'd entrusted to him earlier. Seeing no immediate threat, he handed the rifle to Ashe.

"Hey, what about me?" Frankie appeared from behind him. "I know pretending to be the cops wasn't the most elegant solution, but it was the best I could come up with on short notice."

"You came to help me." Even now, Ashe couldn't quite believe it. "How did you even know I was in trouble?"

Frankie shot a dirty look at Julian. "I couldn't stop thinking about how Marco knew who you were. Someone must have told him. It wasn't me, and it couldn't have been Jesse. Then I thought back to the night of the party, and the last time I saw Jesse before the Diamondbacks showed up." Her lips thinned. *"And who he was with."*

Ashe felt a fresh rush of anger, but along with it came shame. "I owe you an apology . . . for what happened at the barn and for now. I thought you'd betrayed us."

Frankie's expression turned even stonier than when she'd looked at Julian. "I'm not saying I don't understand, but . . . I'd never betray you—or Jesse, or even B.O.B.—like that. I thought you'd know that by now. But I'll give you that one mistake." She locked eyes with Ashe. "Next time you doubt me, I'm done. That's not something I'll forgive twice. Understood?"

Ashe felt her mouth tug up on one side. "It won't happen again."

"Good," said Frankie. "Now let's get out of here. We don't have long before the Diamondbacks realize what they're hearing is a few of my drones making an awful lot of noise."

Ashe checked the ammunition in her rifle. "Not without Jesse."

"Right," said Frankie. "Not without Jesse. But we need to find him fast."

"Good thing we've got someone who knows where he is."

Julian thrashed as B.O.B. lifted him like a toy. "Ashe, Frankie, please! I didn't mean to—"

"I don't care about your excuses," snapped Ashe. "Where's Jesse? Talk fast, Julian. Or B.O.B. here is gonna pop you like a grape."

Julian blanched, then nodded his chin toward a tunnel, opposite the one Marco and the others had taken. "Down there."

The passage was rough-hewn, older feeling than the rest of the hideout. Lit by a string of tepid yellow bulbs, it led them deeper into the stone, past the occasional nook filled with discarded metal parts and old boxes.

"How far?" demanded Ashe, growing increasingly nervous. Every step they took away from the entrance was one they'd have to take back. If the Diamondbacks blocked them in, it was game over.

"I'm not sure," squeaked Julian. "I only saw them take him, not where exactly."

"These old tunnels are like a maze," Frankie said. "We need to—"

A Diamondback appeared from out of a side tunnel, exiting right between Ashe and Frankie. Ashe raised her rifle, but he jumped back, hands raised in surrender.

Bez.

"Don't shoot!" he cried.

"Give me one good reason not to," said Ashe.

Frankie raised a hand. "Ashe, don't!"

At the same time Bez said, "Because I can take you to Jesse."

For a moment, they all stood in wary silence.

"I don't believe you." Ashe kept her rifle ready. "This is a trick. You do what Marco tells you to do."

"I do what's good for the gang." Bez held Ashe's gaze. "Frankie knows that. And right now, what's good for the gang is getting rid of you. Marco has been unhinged ever since you crossed him. It's gotten out of hand."

"You think?" said Frankie.

"We don't have time for this." Ashe nudged Bez with the barrel of the rifle. "If you know where Jesse is, show us. Now."

"Follow me."

He led them deeper into the winding tunnel, moving at a brisk pace until, finally, he stopped before a small side room cut into the rock. A dimly lit holding cell made up half of it, with a wall of iron bars that stretched from floor to ceiling. Inside that cell was a shadowed figure.

Ashe felt some of the tension that gripped her loosen. "Jesse."

Jesse came forward out of the darkness, grinning. "Took you long enough."

But even though he was smiling, one of his eyes was nearly swelled shut, and there was dried blood on his chin from a split lip.

Ashe wheeled on Bez and shoved him into the wall of the cavern. "What did you do to him, you son of a—"

"It wasn't part of the plan!" Bez shouted. "He fought back when we stopped him from warning you at the party."

"That's true," said Jesse. "Don't worry, some of theirs look far worse."

He sounded so nonchalant about it, Ashe could only sigh. She released Bez and turned back to him. "Being behind bars never bothers you, does it, McCree? Take care of this, B.O.B.?"

She took the Viper from the omnic. One arm still wrapped around Julian, B.O.B. drove a fist into the cell's ancient-looking lock, denting it. A few more punches and it gave way, the door swinging open.

Jesse sauntered out. "Nice work, B.O.B." Then his features hardened, eyes narrowing as he glared at Julian. "Gotta admit, I'm tempted to ask you to do the same thing to this traitor."

"L-look, Jesse," Julian stammered. "I was never gonna let them hurt you for real, I swear—"

Jesse raised his fist and swung. Julian's head snapped back, an audible *crunch* sounding as he cried out in pain.

"*That's* what a broken nose feels like," growled Jesse.

Julian tensed, as if expecting another blow, but Jesse simply turned away from him, fists held down at his sides.

"We'll deal with him later." Ashe tossed the Seraphim rifle to Jesse. Antique or not, in that moment the Viper felt right in her hands, like it had been made for her alone. "Thanks," said Jesse. "Though I wish I had my–" B.O.B. reached into a pocket and pulled out the revolver. Jesse's eyes lit up. "Okay, now I'm ready."

"Good," said Ashe. "Time to get out of here, gang."

They headed back the way they'd come, Ashe in the lead, B.O.B. covering the rear. With every step, Ashe expected the Diamondbacks to appear, but they saw no one.

Bez stopped when they reached the corridor where they'd encountered him earlier.

"Where do you think you're going?" said Ashe.

"No one knows I came back to help you." Bez glanced down the side corridor, a worried look on his face. "But if Marco finds out . . ."

"Ashe, just let him go," said Frankie. "We've got Jesse."

"Fine," said Ashe. There was no time to argue. "Go. But if I find out you've told them what happened to us–"

"Not a chance," Bez said with finality. "Marco never should have gotten us mixed up with you in the first place." He turned to Frankie. "Good luck."

Frankie smiled somewhat sadly in response.

Then he was gone. "C'mon." Ashe continued leading them along the main tunnel. "We need to hurry. If any of the Diamondbacks have figured out what's really going on, we'll need a lot more than luck to get out of here in one piece."

CHAPTER 20

When they reached the warehouse again, Frankie's sirens could still be heard. It was a good sign, but Ashe made sure to peek out from the corridor before they exited, just to be sure. She saw no one.

"Wow, those cowards ran and didn't look back," Ashe chuckled. "Nice work, Frankie."

"For all his bluster," said Frankie, "bravery isn't one of Marco's strong suits."

"Let's not hang around to test that," Jesse cut in. "Ashe, want me to take point?"

"You wish." She smirked at him. "I got us into this; I lead us out. Follow me, and keep close."

She exited the tunnel into the warehouse. To her left was the warehouse and loading dock. To her right, the corridor that led to the way out, crates piled up along one side of it. She couldn't see the door from where they were, but she caught a whiff of fresh air as they made their way toward it. All they had to do was get around the corner and they'd be—

"Watch out!" Jesse grabbed her shoulder and yanked, forcing Ashe down a moment before a shot rang out. Bits of concrete rained down from where the bullet hit the wall, showering her.

"Idiot!" Marco cried. Ashe snapped back up in time to catch a glimpse of him, hidden behind the empty shipping container in the loading dock. In an instant, she saw other flashes of movement, rifle barrels appearing from behind crates and around corners. "I said not to hit her! She's the only one still worth anything." Marco had his own rifle, and it was trained on Jesse. "Take out the others, but leave her."

Ashe locked eyes with Jesse. There was no time for a plan. She moved in front of him and raised the Viper. Marco might want her alive, but she was going to make sure the Diamondbacks paid a high price to capture her again.

"Frankie, get behind B.O.B.!" Ashe opened fire on the loading dock. Her first shot was for Marco, who, expecting it, ducked out of sight again. It clanged off the shipping container. "Jesse?"

"I gotcha," Jesse said.

There might not have been time for a plan, but they didn't need one. Moving in sync, Jesse fired around Ashe as they backed toward the exit, targeting the gang members hidden around the warehouse. She heard a yelp as one of her bullets clipped a shoulder, and Jesse crowed with triumph as he picked a revolver right out of one of the Diamondbacks' hands. Ashe glanced over her shoulder just long enough to see Jesse grinning like a madman, and if it hadn't been for the mortal danger, she might have smiled right back. As it was, she felt a rush of excitement. They were closer to the corner now, and after that, they could make a run for the exit.

More shots rang out.

Jesse grunted. "They're behind us!"

Ashe started to turn, then screeched as a line of fire tore across her shoulder. She swore when wet, warm blood began to run down her arm. It was no good. They were surrounded, and if they didn't get some cover quickly . . .

"B.O.B.! Do something!"

The omnic didn't hesitate. He let go of Julian, then dropped one shoulder and charged the crates, colliding with them like a cannon ball. They teetered for a heart-gripping moment before tumbling over, crashing down into haphazard piles.

It wasn't perfect, but it would do. "Everyone take cover!" Ashe yelled.

Frankie and B.O.B., pushing the whimpering Julian, obeyed, ducking behind one of the larger crates. Ashe and Jesse followed, Ashe taking a moment to squeeze off one last round in the direction of the new gunfire. Then she dove behind the makeshift shelter with the others.

Ashe swore. The Diamondbacks had surrounded them, and between the disorienting sirens and the gunfire, she couldn't identify everywhere they'd taken up position. "I think they figured out your ruse, Frankie."

"Guess so." Frankie tapped her hologlasses. The sirens cut off.

"Well, that's a *little* better." Jesse leaned against the crates for support. But he was frowning. "Ashe, you're bleeding."

She looked over at her arm. The fabric of her shirt was soaked red, but the wound wasn't deep. "I'm okay; it's only a graze." But there was a pool of blood on the floor nearby, more than could have come from her. "Where did that– Jesse!"

More blood was pooling beneath the leg of his trousers.

"Yeah," he winced. "They got me, too."

Frankie knelt to examine the injury, a few inches below his

knee. She exhaled with relief. "A flesh wound, but we need to get you some help quick."

"Not a priority," said Jesse, stealing a glance over the pile of crates. "Ashe—"

"I know," she said, looking for herself. There were at least a handful of Diamondbacks still in the loading dock, and more she couldn't see. Plus, whoever had fired at them from the other side. At least two, she guessed, though they were hiding again. Frustration filled her. The door to freedom was right there, less than a hundred steps away.

It might as well have been a mile. "They planned this," she said. "Figured out what Frankie did and then waited until we were out of the tunnel so we couldn't double back. Now we're stuck."

"Yup," said Jesse. "We walked into the trap. Now all they gotta do is close it on us."

"Ashe!" Marco sang out again. "I'm losing my patience with you."

"Yeah, sorry about that!" Ashe cried, trying to buy time to think. "But it was worth it to see the cowardly look on your face when you thought the police were outside."

A moment of annoyed silence passed. "Last chance. Give up and we'll go easy on all of you!"

Ashe didn't believe that for a moment. She might still be worth something if Marco tried to ransom her, but Jesse and Frankie? She looked over at them. "Anyone have any ideas?"

With an ill look, Frankie shook her head. "I've used all of mine."

Jesse had a determined look on his face, but his jaw was tight. "We might be able to shoot our way out, between the two of us."

"No," said Ashe, though it was a tempting thought. "Not with you injured like that. Even with B.O.B. acting as a shield, it's too risky. There's too many of them, and all they need is one lucky shot." She touched the bullet wound on her arm. "And they've already gotten two."

"So . . ." There was a hollowness to the way Jesse said the word. "What do we do?"

Think. Ashe scanned the warehouse around them, her gaze skimming across Jesse and Frankie, B.O.B., even Julian. From where they were stuck, the exit was in view. They could make a run for it. Marco's crew in the warehouse would only have a shot at them for a few seconds, but the ones hunkered down by the doors? They'd have to run right into their line of fire. And even if Marco had ordered them not to hurt Ashe, would they stick to that order as she came at them, guns blazing? Doubtful. Still, one or two of them might make it out . . .

No. That wouldn't work. She wasn't going to gamble with their lives, not even Julian's.

Ashe took a deep breath. As she did, a strange sensation settled over her, easing the tension in her muscles. It wasn't calm, exactly, but rather an understanding. There was no good way out of this.

Not for all of them.

"I've got an idea," Ashe said. "But you're not going to like it."

Jesse's mouth twitched up at one side. "When has that stopped us before?"

"Don't be smart, McCree." Ashe took in that roguish look of his for a moment. Who'd know when, or *if*, she'd see it again? Then she turned away. "Marco! Let's make a deal?"

Silence again. Then: "I'm listening."

"You let the others go and you can have me."

Jesse grabbed her arm. "Ashe, no!"

She shook him off. "They walk out of here, and once they're gone, I come to you. Easy for everyone."

"How do I know you'll keep your word?" called Marco.

"You don't," said Ashe. "Any more than I know you'll keep yours. Guess we'll simply have to trust each other. But a little trust doesn't seem much to ask given how much you think I'm worth in ransom."

There was a long pause. "Okay, you've got a deal."

Ashe turned back to the others.

Frankie was shaking her head. "No, we're not going to leave you."

"Not a chance," said Jesse, sounding angrier than she'd ever heard him.

"Yes, you are." Ashe straightened, jaw set. "This is all my fault. Frankie, we wouldn't even be in this mess if I'd listened to you about Marco. And, Jesse . . ." She felt a strange pang, meeting his eyes. "You made me a promise, when we started all this, remember?"

His face clouded further.

"Remember?" Ashe pressed. "We do things—"

"Your way," he growled. "Yeah, I remember."

Ashe smirked at that. "You're smarter than you look, McCree. My chopper should still be up on the ridge." She reached into her pocket and took out the key chain he'd given her, tossing it to him. "It rides great, by the way. It's a shame we never got a chance to take it out together, but . . ." She shrugged.

"Yeah," said Jesse simply. "A damn shame."

"Get them out of here, as far away as you can."

Jesse opened his mouth to say something, but then closed it again, and nodded. He handed her his rifle. "Take this, just in case."

Ashe shook her head and tightened her grip on the Viper. "No. We don't know whether Marco has anyone outside, too. The antique will do for me just fine. Besides, if he keeps his word, I won't need it."

The lines in Jesse's forehead deepened. "*If* he keeps his word."

"We don't have much choice. Now, get ready." She raised her voice. "Okay, Marco, they're coming out."

Frankie's lip trembled a little. "Good luck, Ashe."

Ashe gave her a little smile. "Thanks again for coming after me."

Jesse said nothing, but he didn't need to. Not at this point.

"Well, hurry up and go," said Marco. "Nobody shoot, ya hear? That's an order!"

Slowly, reluctantly, Jesse and Frankie moved out from behind the crates. Ashe kept them covered as best she could, but if anyone wanted to pick them off, they were easy targets.

"B.O.B."—Ashe kept her eyes on the warehouse—"you too."

"Wait, what about me?" said Julian. The words came out mushy, thanks to Jesse's parting gift.

"Leave him, B.O.B." Ashe shoved him into a corner made by the fallen crates. "You wanted to be a Diamondback, right? Well, now you're stuck."

But B.O.B. still didn't move. He stood, silent, staring at Ashe.

"I know you don't want to go," she said. "But I need you to protect Jesse and Frankie now. Make sure they get away safe." The pair were nearly to the door. Ashe took B.O.B.'s hand—as best she could, given it was five times the size of hers—and squeezed. "Thanks for always being there. Now go."

For a moment, it seemed as if the omnic was thinking hard, torn with indecision. Then B.O.B. turned and clomped after Jesse and Frankie. But Ashe didn't relax until all three were through the exit, and back out into the open air of the gorge. After they disappeared from sight, she counted a minute slowly, afraid at any moment the sound of gunfire would erupt again. But there was nothing.

"Okay, they're gone," said Marco. "You ready to come out now, Ashe?"

"Not quite," she called back. "Thought I'd stay here a tad longer." Every second she bought was another second the others had to get away.

"Don't worry, you take your time." Marco's words turned sly. "Honestly, I thought you'd be a little smarter than this. With McCree and your omnic behemoth, well, maybe one or two of you might have made it out. But now you're split up. How many shots left in that old rifle of yours, Ashe? Not enough, I'd guess. And the moment I've got you in hand, my gang is going after your friends. No one crosses the Diamondbacks and walks away, you hear me?"

"Yeah," Ashe said. But quietly, to herself, "I figured you'd say something like that."

Frankie had warned her, after all. Marco couldn't be trusted. And Marco was dangerous.

Well, he wasn't the only one.

Ashe lunged at Julian. "Hey!" he protested as she rummaged through his pockets until she found what she wanted: the detonator he was supposed to have used earlier.

Julian went paler than ever. "Ashe . . . no."

"Shut up!" She glanced out at the loading dock again. "Hey, Marco, I gotta question for you: Do you see Julian's bike there, sitting right in the middle of your hideout? And do you see the crate on the back of it? Well, that crate is filled with dynamite."

"Oh yeah?" said Marco. "What are you getting at, Ashe?"

Something she didn't really want to be getting at, but desperate times . . . "Well, only that it's an awful lot of explosives . . . and I'm holding the detonator."

Silence.

"What do you think, Marco? Julian's the expert, but I'm pretty sure that's enough to bring down a few hundred tons of rock on top of all of us."

"You're lying!" Marco said, a satisfying hint of worry in his voice.

"Am I?" said Ashe. "You said it yourself: No one crosses the Diamondbacks and walks away. Well, I'm not going to let you hurt my gang—my family—no matter what it takes."

Beside her, Julian let out a little noise like a trapped animal.

"You'd be buried, too," taunted Marco.

"Like I said," Ashe replied, entirely calm, "no matter what it takes. And in case any of y'all hiding near the exit are getting ideas, if I see anyone make a run for it, I press this button."

"Ashe!" yelled Marco. "I swear if this is a bluff—"

Julian was shaking. "She's not bluffing, Marco!" His voice cracked as he yelled. "Ashe doesn't bluff! She'll blow us all to kingdom come!"

Ashe almost laughed. "Better listen to him, Marco. Trust me, things go better when folks listen to me." She should have been scared, but adrenaline rushed through her veins, and for some reason, she couldn't stop herself from smiling.

The question was, what now? She could make them all throw down their guns and come out, maybe manage to round them up somehow. But where would that leave her, especially if she missed one? And even if she got away safe, the Diamondbacks were sure to hold a grudge. And that was the last thing Ashe wanted. She needed to deal with them now. Because if she'd learned anything from the last few months, it was that it was better to have friends than enemies.

"Y'know," she called out, loud enough to make sure she was heard throughout the hideout. "None of this would have happened if Marco hadn't been greedy. And mean. Which makes me wonder why exactly any of you follow him in the first place."

No one said anything.

"Now, if you were part of my crew, it wouldn't be like that. *My* crew gets treated with respect, and gets equal shares of whatever we steal. Isn't that right, Julian?"

Julian's fear turned to surprise. "Uh, yeah."

"And there's none of this fighting with other gangs over scraps," Ashe continued. "There's plenty to go around, if you plan things right. And I always do. Plus, my gang throws great parties—you've all seen that. So, forget about my deal with Marco. Here's a deal for the rest of you: Join up with me. No one gets shot, no one gets blown up, and we all walk away from this better than when we started. 'Cept, Marco, of course. You'll need to do something about him."

"What?" Marco sounded about ready to burst. "If any of you even think about—"

"Ashe is right." It was Bez. Ashe couldn't quite tell where he was, but apparently, he hadn't run off after helping rescue Jesse. "You got us into this mess, Marco. You've gotten us into a lot of messes lately. You've only managed to stay in charge because you kick around the rest of us. That's why

Frankie left. Well, I've seen how Ashe runs her outfit, and it's a hell of a lot better than this. Ashe, I'm in!"

A brief silence passed.

Then: "The hell with this," someone else said. "If Bez is joining up with Ashe, I am, too."

"Me too," came another voice.

Ashe exhaled with relief as other voices chimed in. Then, suddenly, came the sounds of a scuffle.

"Hey! Stop, don't you—" Marco cried out, only to be cut off suddenly.

Ashe waited for the activity to settle, then peeked around the side of the crates. Farther back in the warehouse stood Bez, rifle raised, along with most of the Diamondbacks. They surrounded Marco, unarmed and on his knees, as well as a handful of others, including Zeke.

"Come on out, Ashe," said Bez, a satisfied look on his face. "You've got yourself a deal."

For a moment, Ashe hesitated, wary of a trick. But then Bez's words came back to her: *I do what's good for the gang.* Plus, he had helped save Jesse, and Frankie trusted him. Still, she kept the detonator in clear sight as she moved out from behind the crates, using the Viper to push Julian in front of her like a shield.

No one moved as she approached. Not even Marco, who looked like he was chewing on a lemon. Ashe nodded at

Bez and the Diamondbacks who'd revolted. "Y'all made the right choice. Now"–she motioned toward the open shipping container nearby–"put them in there until I figure out what to do with them."

Marco's face was deep red with rage by the time they were herded inside. "You traitors," he growled. "You dirty traitors. You're all going to regret this. You especially, Ashe. I swear, you leave me alive and I'll–"

"Oh, be quiet." Ashe used the barrel of the Viper to shove Julian inside the shipping container, right into Marco. "You keep spouting off about what happens to people who cross the Diamondbacks, Marco, when you should have been worrying more about what happens when *you* cross *me*."

With that, Ashe slammed the door of the container shut, and barred it. Immediately came the sound of fists pounding on metal, and cries of anger, but she ignored them.

Instead, she stuck the detonator in her pocket and held out her hand to Bez. "Welcome aboard."

He smiled and shook. "Thanks . . . boss."

"I only have one rule," Ashe said, addressing them all. "We do things my way. Understand?" They all nodded immediately. "Good. Then first things first. Bez, you go get Frankie and Jesse and B.O.B. They can't have gotten too far yet. As for the rest of you"–they snapped to attention– "get this place cleaned up. I want an inventory of guns and supplies in my hand in an hour. And somebody put that dynamite somewhere safe."

A few minutes ago, they'd been trying to capture her. Now, every one of the Diamondback defectors began to move, eager to obey her directions. Ashe smirked. This wasn't exactly where she'd expected her crime spree to lead, but she wasn't at all disappointed. In fact, the possibilities were already flying through her mind.

Yes, this could work out just fine indeed.

Viper in hand, Ashe made her way to the entrance of the hideout, back out into Deadlock Gorge. As the warm sun hit her, she closed her eyes and tilted her face toward it, taking a deep breath and letting it out again. Her heart still pounded in her chest, and the graze on her arm was throbbing painfully, but this was the best she'd felt in ages.

Spoiled rich girl.

Troublemaker.

Thief.

Gang leader.

She'd been a lot of things lately, and with every title, someone—her parents, the law, or a rival gang—had tried to control her, tear her down, or break her.

But she hadn't been controlled. She hadn't been broken. Each time, she'd come out on top.

And Elizabeth Caledonia Ashe was just getting started.

Sheriff Carson looked up at the light knock. One of his deputies stood in the doorway to his office.

"Uh, Sheriff," the deputy said, an uncertain look on his face. "Something just arrived for you."

A package? He wasn't expecting anything. "Well, bring it in."

"Sorry, Sheriff," said the deputy. "I can't. It's too big."

Too big?

The sheriff stood and followed the deputy to the front door of the station. Outside, a large shipping container sat in the street, an envelope taped to it. It was addressed to him.

Dear Sheriff Carson.

I know I've been a thorn in your side before, and while I'd love to promise that will never be the case again, I'm pretty sure I'd be lying. So, here's a gift from me to you, one that I hope will settle things between us, at least for a little while. Included below is information for where you can transfer the reward for their capture. Don't make me ask for it twice.

—Ashe

EPILOGUE

Ashe poured a generous amount of milk into her coffee, certain it would do nothing to improve the awful taste. The pie wasn't much better, judging by the look on Frankie's face across the table. It was just as well they hadn't come here for the food. They sat in the nearly deserted Panorama Diner, serenaded by a jukebox that didn't seem to have a single song that had been made in either of their lifetimes. B.O.B. was nearby, nearly taking up a whole booth of his own, hands folded neatly on the table. Ashe couldn't help but be a little jealous. No one expected omnics to order anything. Across from him, Bez sat hunched over a pile of paper, making occasional notes or scratching something out with a pencil.

She sighed and scooped a spoonful of sugar into her mug, despite having no intention of drinking the foul concoction. "Hey, Bez, how's recruitment coming?"

"Not bad," he said. "Members of a bunch of other local gangs have been coming around, looking to join up. I'll let you know when I have a list for you to look at."

"Good." Ashe nodded. "Let's hope a few of them know their way around a heist."

Meanwhile, Frankie's eyes tracked something only she could see in her hologlasses. "We're going to need to order more equipment for the new recruits." She laughed. "You should read some of the stories they're telling around Bellerae about what happened to the Diamondbacks. You've got some fans out there, Ashe."

"Is that so?"

Suddenly, the bell over the diner door tinkled and Jesse stumbled in, arms piled high with brown paper packages.

"You're late," grumbled Ashe as he dumped them on the table, barely missing both the coffee and the pie.

"Sorry." Jesse sounded nothing of the sort.

"So?" Ashe pressed. "How do they look?"

"Pretty good." Jesse doled out the packages as Bez and B.O.B got up and came over. "One for you, Frankie, Bez, and one for me." He tossed the largest bundle to the omnic. "And B.O.B., of course."

Ashe immediately tore open the paper on hers, revealing a red jacket, and the silvery winged skull insignia that filled its back side.

Deadlock Rebels.

They'd come up with the name together. Well, mostly she and Jesse. B.O.B. hadn't had much to contribute, and Frankie and Bez were too busy working on the gang's next jobs to give it much thought. But it was an apt name, given they'd decided to take over the Diamondbacks' old hideout in Deadlock Gorge. Seemed a shame to waste it, since it had already been set up so nicely. There'd been no complaints from the locals, either, who seemed perfectly content to get rid of Marco in favor of the new tenants.

In the center of the lettering was their insignia, a skull with a pair of sharp, sweeping wings and a—

Bez held up his jacket with a confused look on his face. "Why does it say *established 1976*?"

Jesse gave Ashe a knowing smile. The chopper. Like their gang, it had started off in pieces, and become so much more.

Ashe coughed, "Never mind that now."

"Lookin' good, B.O.B.," said Frankie, as the omnic put his vest on.

The omnic tipped his bowler to her, the hat going just fine with the new look.

"It's official, then. From this day forward, we're the Deadlock Rebels." Ashe looked around at the faces surrounding her. They'd worked with her, planned with her, fought with her; hell, they'd even saved her life. And seeing them now, gathered and wearing their new insignia for the first time, triggered a strange feeling, one that was so unfamiliar it took her a moment to identify it.

Home. This felt like home.

"But more than a gang," she continued, "we're a family. And like a real family, once you're in Deadlock, you're in it for life."

Jesse grinned. "Deadlock for life."

"For life," echoed Frankie and Bez.

B.O.B. didn't say anything, but it was clear he felt the same. At least to Ashe.

"Then let's get going, gang. That shipment will be along soon." Ashe stood, slipped her vest on, and grabbed the Viper from the seat beside her. As she settled her hat on her head, she smirked at her new family. "And it ain't gonna steal itself."

ACKNOWLEDGMENTS

Thank you to the Overwatch team at Blizzard for giving me the opportunity to write within their fantastic universe, something the college-aged, Diablo II-obsessed me never would have believed she'd get to do someday. It was an honor and pleasure to get to work with Ashe and the gang.

Special thanks to Lori and Chloe for helping me wrangle this story and get it where it needed to go, as well as to my literary agent Laura, for all of her invaluable help and advice.

And finally, thanks to all my geeky, gamer friends who keep me going with their unflagging friendship and support. I hope they, along with the rest of the Overwatch fans out there, have as much fun reading this book as I did writing it. (Especially you, A.R.L.)